"Stop!" he did not even have to raise his voice, she was so attuned to his desires. She turned. "Come here," in a soft voice.

She closed the door again and obeyed. He unbuttoned the white, sand-stained blouse gently, then with a sudden wrench, tore the expensive American bra— one of her indulgences—ripping the shoulder straps and snapping the front clasp. Her heavy brown nippled breasts tumbled free again. He ripped the remainders of the garment off, and dropped them to the floor, then knelt at her feet. His hand came up under skirt, ripped off her panties, shredding them in his powerful hands.

"Go now. I am Orpheo. A vahine, *my* vahine, does not wear such…things. Tomorrow, after work." He dismissed her, watching as she walked out the door, her hips swaying. The morning sun was up, and she knew that for the rest of the day she would be conscious of people watching her heavy naked breasts under the blouse.

Also by N. Whallen:
Compliance

TAU'TEVU

N. WHALLEN

MASQUERADE BOOKS, INC.
801 SECOND AVENUE
NEW YORK, N.Y. 10017

Tau'tevu
Copyright © 1996 by N. Whallen
All Rights Reserved

No part of this book may be reproduced, stored in a retrieval system, or transmitted in any form, by any means, including mechanical, electronic, photocopying, recording or otherwise, without prior written permission of the publishers.

First Masquerade Edition 1996

First Printing August 1996

ISBN 1-56333-426-7

Manufactured in the United States of America
Published by Masquerade Books, Inc.
801 Second Avenue
New York, N.Y. 10017

Chapter 1

His name was Orpheo. He had come to Tau'tevu from somewhere. Perhaps he had a passport that indicated where he was from, but as he slid through the crowds in the main streets, under the overhangs, passing the tourists, there was no indication of any of it. Neither the warm humid air nor the cool of the trade winds seemed to change either his sardonic sharp expression or the cool strength of his dark body.

Vivian—her birth name was V'iaroaa'ave'ahine—finished her day's work at the Department of Transport and stepped off the verandah into the cooling deep afternoon. The winds were beginning to sigh in the palm trees overhead and she automatically moved out of the reach of any falling nut. Tau'tevu stretched around her. The babble of English, Hindi, *Kanak*, and the blur of brown and white faces. Behind her she could hear John Malafuni, her boss, singing quietly to himself as he finished his paperwork for the day. He was a good boss, notwithstanding his habit of grabbing her ass whenever they were alone in an attempt to get her to join him on the beach one night. She would have too, but for his wife, ten children, two or three regular girlfriends, and sixty-five years of life. And he had a wonderful voice.

She was pure *kanak*. Frizzy hair puffed up in what would have been called an afro elsewhere, but was just *kanak* on Tau'tevu. Beneath it lay almost six feet of muscular young woman. A large rib cage supported firm large breasts and was bolstered by broad, even heavy, hips. She had the light golden brown coloration of the true native.

Vivian wondered what to do with the rest of the day. She took a breath, sighed, and turned towards Kimball's. Like most of the ocean front places, it was crowded by Australian tourists. Vulgar and loud. But she needed a beer after the day's work. And she could ignore the bastards. Sometimes—rarely enough, when the loneliness hit her—she would allow herself to be picked up. And even, if the bloody tourist were not too drunk, or crude, or smelly with beer and sweat (didn't those people *ever* wash?), she would allow one to fuck her. Or not. Several times she had fought off overzealous lovers, once by punching the man in the balls. She had seen him later, bent over and staring at nothing, and his hands had cupped his crotch protectively as she passed by. She had smiled and moved on. Once she had been raped by a coldly drunken tourist, on the beach, after they had some beers at a café. The memory flushed her cheeks with hot anger, and yet with a tingle between her legs that she could not ignore.

Tau'tevu

She watched the *kanak* men as she passed. They, like the Australian and other tourists did not live up to her expectations either, expecting a woman to do their work, wanting to marry, have kids, be waited on hand and foot.

She sat sipping her beer, enjoying the breeze, ignoring the stares and meant-to-be overheard comments of the Aussie man when she noticed him. He sat erect in the chair, forearms on the table cradling a gin sling. His eyes had been scanning the crowd, moving methodically from one side of the large saloon to the other. His gaze crossed hers and he *looked* at her. His smooth almost round face—too pale to be a *kanak*, too dark to be an Aussie—bore an inscrutable expression. His unblinking eyes held hers for a moment. They dropped to the curve of her blouse, neither furtively, as most men did, nor challenging as some. He looked at her hands, one holding the beer glass, the other playing with the string of her necklace, its strung shark's teeth clinking softly. He held her gaze for a long moment until she turned away, overpowered by his eyes. When she dared look again, he was gone. She finished her beer, walked out. A large hand took her elbow.

"Come," he said. He had dark eyes, and a vague, male musky smell—clean and enticing—touched her nostrils. They walked through the gloom of the poorly lit streets: two large self-confident people. Overlooking the beach he stopped at the entrance to a luxurious bungalow. Vivian recognized it as belonging to the Sea Spray Hotel: Tau'tevu's only real luxury hotel.

For a second she contemplated escape. She knew nothing of this man. He was clean smelling, yes, and well built, but there was a cruel sensual cut to his mouth, and hidden depths in what she had seen of his eyes. His hand rose, anticipating her objections, and rested on her shoulder. The flesh yielded beneath the pressure of iron-vise fingers. The pain was brutal, then suddenly he dropped his hand. She was in the process of telling him to stop, and the sudden cessation of pain brought with it a flush of disappointment so intense she cried out. Still looking at her, he stepped through the open door and stopped, waiting for her to make up her mind.

Her head swirling with thoughts and half-formed dreams, Vivian followed.

"You are in my house," he said, translating the native greeting into English. Vivian nodded. "I am happy," she responded. She trembled as she said it. Both knew that the standard greetings had achieved new meanings.

He turned on the light, keeping it dim with the wall rheostat. Moving slowly, irresistibly, he clasped both her shoulders with his warm palms. Her muscles felt like soft jelly. His lips brushed her mouth, the hint of teeth felt under the flesh. She heard a faint sound and knew his pants had hit the floor. Pushed by his hands, she resisted the attempt and found herself hooked by ankles and falling onto the reed-mat covered floor. The mat was the finest the luxury hotel could buy, and it cushioned her fall well, but the sudden descent of his body on hers drove the breath from her lungs. She resisted wordlessly but powerfully, pushing at his shoulders, biting his neck. His hands pinned her to the mat while his powerful hips insinuated him between her legs. Vivian snarled happily, not aiding him in any way. She was conscious of the warm tip of his cock nuzzling at her entrance, pushing past the leg of her panties, then she shrieked softly but uncontrollably as with one strong lunge he buried his maleness in her to the hairs. Vivian sighed happily. It was like her dreams, the force, the power of his movements. He did not ask nor beg, nor had he forced her. He had simply taken what was his and granted her her own.

The man set to work fucking her, his body arching over the bowl of her thighs, forcing himself deeply in, pulling back until she could feel the rim of his cockhead. His blunt hard hands held her shoulders pinned to the mat, and she could see the glimmer of his white teeth hovering over her.

Not waiting for her, though she was very close, he climaxed. Spurts of thick stuff coated her insides. She trembled, cried, hoping for her own release, but he ignored her unspoken demands completely. His cock still pulsing, the end flow still emerging from the tip, he withdrew from her, rose to his feet and pulled her up after him.

He walked them to the bed. She stood for a moment, the frustration in her face plain to see even in the dim light, her dark full hair tangled with sweat.

"Undress," he said briefly. When she failed to respond he reached for the top button of her blouse. Vivian noted suddenly that though he had come, his cock was still fully erect. She undressed rapidly, and he watched with lazy eyes, still standing before her. He made no attempt to grab at her as she stripped, not even when she provocatively swayed from foot to foot dropping her cotton panties.

She lay back on the large bed, spreading her legs. He stood there watching her. Then she understood, rising from the bed, she stripped him of his expensive shirt, undid his sandals. Then she rose to stand against him, the prominent areas of their two bodies touching, her eyes on his face.

Deliberately, and with no malice, he slapped her face on either side. Hard. A red veil rose in front of her eyes. She wanted to rip out his eyes, but was too shocked to move. The penetration of his hard, erect prick into her gluey cunt took her by surprise but suddenly she was climaxing inexorably, driven by the intensity of her outrage and pain, and the surprising penetration. She would have screamed but that his cruel mouth was already on hers, sucking the scream and the rage away, leaving her awash with the slowly receding waves of orgasm. She sagged in his arms, was vaguely conscious of his still erect prick withdrawing from her cunt, an audible "plop" sound as it withdrew completely. A trail of wetness made its way down the insides of her thighs. She opened her eyes again. Her cheeks were unnaturally warm, cooled by his palms which had emerged from over her shoulders to cup her face. His eyes, fierce and blank as a shark's, were looking into hers.

"Warrior," she said, understanding. He stood massively by as she pulled on her clothes and turned to the door. She brushed by him, conscious of the shock of energy that passed between them. The wood felt electric to her fingers as she opened the door.

"Stop!" he did not even have to raise his voice, she was so attuned to his desires. She turned. "Come here," in a soft voice.

She closed the door again and obeyed. He unbuttoned the white, sand-stained blouse gently, then with a sudden wrench, tore the expensive American bra—one of her indulgences—ripping the shoulder straps and snapping the front clasp. Her heavy brown nippled breasts tumbled free again. He ripped the remainders of the garment off, and dropped them to the floor, then knelt at her feet. His hand came up under skirt, ripped off her panties, shredding them in his powerful hands.

"Go now. I am Orpheo. A vahine, *my* vahine, does not wear such...things. Tomorrow, after work." He dismissed her, watching as she walked out the door, her hips swaying. The morning sun was up, and she knew that for the rest of the day she would be conscious of people watching her heavy naked breasts under the blouse.

Chapter 2

The sea breezes were whispering through the coconut palms when she reached the bungalow again. There was no question in her mind that she would be there, no doubt at all. The pulse hammered heavily in her chest, her nipples so hard they hurt with every step. And between her thighs she felt a growing wetness, an uncontrolled shuddering of anticipation.

Vivian took one last look at the beach and the sea and pushed the door open. The lights were low again.

"I am here," she called out the familiar greeting. There was no answer. There was a faint frisson of doubt in her mind, but something, the taste of the air, the tenseness of her body, some barely heard sound told her that he was there, waiting, like some great shark waiting in the deep.

She walked boldly into the living room. The well-woven mat swallowed the sound of her footsteps. The room was empty. She passed through it to the bedroom that was hidden by a curtain of woven fibers—a specialty of the island. The room, with its large double bed was empty too, though the light was on dimly. She wondered whether to undress, what to do, and in the end, merely stood there, patiently waiting for what would come.

The sound, when it came, was a sudden shock. Something hissed through the air. She wanted to leap and run, but her control came to her aid and she merely turned slowly, her eyes large.

He stood there, his phallus a massive jutting pillar in the dim light. He was naked but for a shark-tooth necklace supporting a whale tooth, and woven armbands. They must have cost a fortune she thought, then she thought, "How dare he wear such things? They are only for chiefs!" Then she realized how misplaced was her outrage. And not because he was not an islander.

He raised his hand. Clenched in his fist was a mass of thin strands. Smooth fibers, the kind used for the weaving of the softer kinds of mats. Her skin quailed, though a fountain of expectant joy was growing like a volcano in her middle. She looked at him through rounded eyes, deeper than forest pools and as quiet.

Orpheo nodded in satisfaction, just a slight inclination of his head. He approached closer and again she was conscious of the muskiness of his body scent, and she breathed it in deeply. His hands gently stroked her cheek, hesitating briefly over the tiny scars on her cheeks from a long-forgotten case of chicken pox. She was sensitive to the ugliness of the scars and started uneasily. His hand stayed, briefly, inquiring at the spot, and moved on approvingly, only when she quieted again.

She was wearing a plain white blouse under a blue blazer, and conservative navy skirt to match. Her skin, that had been icy cold as she approached his room, had warmed now, and she waited, expectantly, for it to heat even more.

For a brief moment his hand stopped at her throat, one finger stroking an earlobe, the thumb resting in the hollow of her throat. She knew, even when it tightened, that it was not a real threat, a real move, and then she saw his face watching her, expressionless, and knew, knew without doubt, that if she resisted, the hand would clench around her vulnerable soft flesh. She shivered deliciously at the knowledge that there was no going back.

The hand drifted down her smooth brown skin to the top button of her spotless white blouse. His left hand, crooked slightly behind him, still held the traditional *muloko'ewa*, the whip-strand used to subdue a reluctant woman. Chiefs had decreed their use in the old days, as a minor punishment for domestic infractions. It had long since been banished, together with much else of Tau'tevan culture, when the colonial masters had come. *They* preferred to be the only ones wielding whips.

The button was undone, flashing briefly in the light as it twisted in his fingers. The hand drifted downwards once again, a second button followed. Vivian could feel the pressure of her large, heavy breasts straining against the fabric. Her nipples had been rubbed pleasingly against it all day, while she sat at work waiting for the evening. He pulled the tails of her blouse out of her waistband and her breasts pushed forward. She bowed her shoulders, teasing him with her movements. His hands rose and Orpheo slapped her hard on the soft mounds, with a motion so fast she could not tell the movement of the first slap from that of the second.

"Vahine," he said in measured tones. "You are mine, you stand straight and proud, with your shoulders back. You do not humble yourself!"

She drew herself up, though the fierceness of the blows had brought tears to her eyes and the desire to curl up and hide herself from the pain. Orpheo continued, dropping her jacket off her shoulders and onto the floor. She wanted to sigh in relief—the jacket was hot—but knew he would not approve. Her blouse was on the floor at her feet, a pale puddle of fabric, soon obscured by her dark skirt, which slid down her thighs with a tired susurrus as he undid the catches at the waistband.

Using his palms, slid flat on her skin, Orpheo followed the contours of her body. Not so much stroking it as making them known to one another—hands, meet Vivian, Vivian meet hands—and tasting her scent and sweat. She shivered but did not change her stance when his wide palms encircled the tops of her thighs, the tip of each middle finger reaching to the fullness of her buttocks, each thumb poised in the softer area of the inside of her thigh. She bore the grip without a murmur as his thumbs dug into the flesh, squeezing her thick thighs, the thighs she was half ashamed of, creating twin bruise marks between her legs. The *muloko'ewa* hung from a loop around his wrist, the grass strands tickling her knees and promising much to come. She moaned, not in fear or pain, though those were there too, but in concern less she faint and lose some of the wild sensations of pleasure and pain that shot through her.

Vivian staggered when he released her thighs. Swift as a snake he was upon her. His right hand grasped her breast heartlessly and propelled her toward the bed. Then he was behind her, one hand entwined in the lush long hair of her head, the other grasping her shoulder, and she was face down on the bed that smelled of fresh sheets, yet paradoxically of a wild man. He pulled her legs apart roughly until her feet hung over the edges of the bed on either side. She knew she was completely exposed there. Then he leaned over her back, and for a brief, panic stricken moment, she thought that that would be all: soon he would enter her and it would be over. Instead, he pulled her wrist out until it touched the bedpost on the far side. She clutched at the wood, and did the same on the other corner when he directed her hand there.

From that uncomfortable position she watched as he readied himself, transferring the lash to his right, measuring her back with a steady glance.

Without haste his hand rose, then descended in a flash. For a brief, suspended instant of time, her skin did not know what had happened to it. Then fire sprang up on her buttocks, they roiled in pain. Her hips tried to squirm, to get away from the fiery agony. Knowing what was to come, Vivian had steeled herself for the pain, but her body wanted away, away, and it took all she had to keep her muscles and skin in place. The look of respect and appreciation on Orpheo's face was reward enough.

He raised his hand once again, and again lashed her

across her full ass. She tried not to scream, not to beg him to cease. A strangled grunt escaped her lips nonetheless. Then the blows started landing with metronomic precision. Her buttocks writhed helplessly, but she divorced herself from her errant skin, digging strong fingers deeply into the cover of the bed, grinding her full tits deeply into the bed, her inflamed nipples soothed by the rough treatment.

"What will you do to me?" she wailed in a low voice, feigning panic.

"I will do what a chief does," he answered remotely.

"Yes," she said dreamily. Her insides were twitching expectantly. Images of fierce warriors forcing themselves onto female flesh, of women dancing around captives tied supine in defeat, flitted through her mind.

She heard a deep throated sound behind her, a sound that rose in cadence with the beating and her own helpless grunts. He was chanting as he beat her, an eerie deep melody that followed the blazing stripes that laced her skin. She knew, in the depths of her mind, that it was the song of victory, the song of a chief who has subdued another's woman and was taking his pleasure from her. She smiled deeply in the depths of her agony.

Orpheo suddenly dropped the lash. He grasped her lacerated buttocks. The touch was a touch of fire, trickling through her skin to the very depths of her spin. His grip forced her around, rolled her over on the bed until she was looking up at his mask-like face.

She could feel a wetness between her thighs, and knew that it was not from the stripes on her buttocks. Her cunt was blazing with desire. Its moisture and softness belied her hard and painful behind. And she knew that there was only one thing missing. She parted her legs, raising her hips, her eyes staring deeply into those of her tormentor.

Orpheo pulled her hair back until she felt the strain on her neck and the cords in her throat stood out. Her heels dug into the bedding, her knees spread wide, bracing her body. When she felt she could not hold the pose any longer, he slipped a triangular bolster under her arched back. Still holding her hair he bent forward and kissed her savagely. His tongue penetrated between her lips and his own mouth ground against her mouth ferociously, as if to drink her in. She could feel his lingual exploration of her mouth, and rather than lying passively back, she fought against the invasive presence with her tongue as best she could. Their tongues intertwined, slithered against one another, and she could taste the marvelous male taste of his body. Then he pulled back, and as if in acknowledgment of his efforts, kissed her lightly but firmly, without forcing her in any way. She responded in kind, gently returning the kiss, while ignoring the screams of her arched spine and burning scalp.

Orpheo righted himself. He removed his hand from her hair, and she lay, still in the same pose, waiting for his next move. The sight of his beautiful male body brought a dryness to her throat. He was fully erect, and for the first time she had the leisure, if only briefly, to examine his maleness. It rose, purple brown stalk, to the level of his deep navel. A thicket of curly, brown hair sheltered its root, and below it hung a small ball sack, pulsing with life.

"It is so beautiful," Vivian said, her breath coming in rapid, shallow draughts.

"Look carefully," he said savagely. "Soon it will be inside you, soon you will feel its *mana* coursing through your channels.

She licked her lips, and could only repeat, "So beautiful, my chieftain, so beautiful."

He allowed her the luxury of admiring him for a brief moment, then bent over the junction of her thighs. The dark brown lips were sealed against his gaze, and while she could not see what he was doing, she could imagine his actions by the feel of his hands on her.

Orpheo examined the juncture of the brown legs for a luxuriously long moment. Then he bent down and savagely pulled apart the full, long, outer lips.

"You have not been a virgin for a long time. That is good," he said, inserting his fingers deeply into her. "You will be able to stand much."

She moaned in pain, and he moved his fingers brutally so that now he had pulled her pussy completely open, exposing the pink inside hole as wide as it would go. The inner membranes were glistening in the light, and the dark musky smell of the woman was overpowering. His head descended and his mouth filled with her wet flesh. He drove his tongue deeply into the waiting hole while pulling hard at the labia, parting them even more. He heard her grunting, and at first her hips, held high by the bolster, seemed to shrink from him. Then, as her moans grew louder, she forced her hips up, to meet the savaging of his mouth and tongue. His teeth came into play, grazing the sensitive parts of her inner lips. She was grunting and her heels dug deeply into the bedding.

He released her for a moment, then stood back, reaching behind him for what he needed. Vivian drew a shuddering breath, and her soft large breasts, spread over her strong rib cage quivered. Orpheo climbed back on the bed. He squatted before her head. His scrotum dangled, a hairy fine mass, over her chin. He gripped the root of his stem and bent it downwards while fumbling between his thighs and finally holding on to the mass of tightly curled black hair that spilled from her head. The soft spongy head of his penis trailed over Vivian's throat and chin, then waited at the entrance to her open mouth. She licked her lips quickly, ready for him. The slight shift in the muscles of his thighs prepared her for the onslaught, as Orpheo shoved his cock down her mouth. It seemed to penetrate her forever, reaching to her throat. She wanted to gag and throw the invading member out, but disciplined herself, as she knew he expected her to, and let it slide past her glottis. She could breath, but barely, and she waited patiently for his next move. He pulled back, then moved forward into her, the most intimate penetration she had ever felt. Out and in again he moved, his excitement palpable by the tension in his body, while she lay passive, dreamy.

Orpheo's hands stroked her full breasts, pinching the nipples painfully but not harshly. He explored the domed curve of her brown stomach, the hollows outside and above her hipbones. Vivian felt all this, wondering where it was leading to. As the pulsing started in his cock, as she thought he would erupt, disappointingly, in the depths of her throat, he pulled back. She sipped gratefully at the wonderful salty taste of his liquor, grateful that she had found a lover with that great a control. She luxuriated in the taste of the spongy mass in her mouth.

There was movement above her, and she had a brief

crack of time to prepare for the sound of a magnified ripping sound, and then the stripe from the lash caught her full across her mounded belly. She screamed, helpless to control her reaction. Her mouth opened wide and he used the time to rock himself forward into her oral cavity once again. Her jaws snapped together, and she felt her teeth graze the skin of his shaft, then managed, barely, to restrain her urge to bite deeper.

Orpheo felt the cut of her large teeth into his member. The sensation of danger was palpable, and he had taken a calculated risk. He raised the quirt again and brought it down full on Vivian's rounded belly. A welt sprang up and her stomach muscles writhed. Two parallel strokes fell, one after the other, on her broad hipbones and she cried out, the sound muffled by his glans, but sending a unique vibration through his frame. He dug the fingers of his left hand full into her vulva, raising her hips higher than before, then struck onto her exposed and prominent mound. Her cry was louder but she did not so much as move her head. The pain of the lash whose tip had grazed his palm added to his feeling. He struck but once again, knowing that they were both near the limit, and then his cock gave a massive pulse, flooding her mouth with his cream. Her own belly writhed in a complicated dance. Her interior was suddenly flooded with the juices of her own passion and waves of an orgasm, the sort that had never happened to her before, racked her frame to an insensate peak of feeling.

Vivian came to herself to the feel of a thin stream of come dripping past the corner of her eye. He helped her by sliding the bolster out from under her and she collapsed gratefully onto the rumpled bedding. He handed her a batik-dyed fabric which, she knew, had cost a fair sum at Patel's. She disdained it, brushing the drops of his essence into her mouth, tasting the leftovers of his passion.

He looked down at her, sitting soft and replete before him, one knee drawn up, the other on the bed. Her breasts, full and brown, hid the stripes down her belly and sides. She smiled happily up at him, then looked around the bungalow room.

As if divining her thoughts, Orpheo said, "I have taken the estate on Taulea Point."

She nodded. She knew the place. Old Ta had owned the place, and always refused to part with it because it was reputed to be a place of *mana*. She wondered how he had managed to convince the old man, but knew it to be a foolish speculation. He was himself, she knew.

He bent and kissed her on her lips. "Go," he said. "There are things to be done." She rose to dress.

Chapter 3

It was an indolent afternoon. Sunday. In the morning she had had to suffer another family get-together. The men sipped *kava*, the mild narcotic numbing the lips. Someone produced a guitar and sang, and the old people and some of the kids danced. The aunties twitted her about not being married. In the end, to silence the hints and outright attempts at matchmaking she simply said, looking around with obvious contempt, that she had yet to find a *real* man. This led, not unexpectedly, to cackles of delight among the older generation, and tales of their sexual adventures in youth and not-so-youth. Vivian slipped away after lunch, still wearing the flower and pandanus wreath, her hands smelling faintly of coconut oil.

He had known she was on her way. It was always so with him, she noticed. It was not that he never went out: when she called on the phone, his bungalow was empty more times than not. But when she came, he was always there.

Orpheo stood on the mat in the middle of the room. He was completely naked and his erection jutted forward and up, curved like a horn, waiting for her. She walked up to him, her bare feet sliding on the mats. Orpheo raised a lazy hand and grasped the full mass of dark hair at the top of her head. His face was a frozen mask and her heart thumped noisily at the sight. He pushed downwards and she sank gracefully to her knees. The knob of his cock butted at her lips. Her mouth opened and he pushed the spongy mass inside.

"My *vahine*," he said as he pushed forward. "Your mouth is well trained. That is good."

She could feel the weight of it against her tongue for a brief moment before he pushed forward. She started to gag, and two rough blows caught her cheeks, making them flame, raising her anger to a blazing fire.

"You are not a child! Persevere! Show me you are worthy! You are not a weak little aunt but a woman worthy of a warrior!"

She was angry, she suddenly realized, furious at the old aunties, at the whole stupid clan who did not know how to behave, at their indolence. They were feared man-eaters, once. The islands around Tau'tevu feared the men of Tau'tevu for their ferocity and their magic. Now they were nothing. Orpheo rammed into her again, then started using her mouth for his pleasure. She tried to suck at the gagging morsel, but he would have none of that. He slapped her again, and with each blow, her temper rose, and with it, her lust.

He stiffened suddenly, and the preliminary drops of

his essence touched her tongue, then there was a sudden pulsing along the warm fleshtube and her mouth was flooded with the bitter taste of his juices as he emptied himself into her.

He drew away from her, and roughly threw her onto her back on the matting. "Captive!" he snarled, using the traditional word which meant humiliation and shame to those captured.

The mat scratched pleasantly at her back and behind. Dragging her by the hair, he pulled her closer to one of the small tables in the room. He knelt with one knee keeping her captive, digging into her stomach beneath her breasts.

"You will not escape," he said, and she knew it was not a threat, merely a statement of fact which transcended anything she could do.

She started to flail about until his hands grasped hers. Her arms were tied swiftly behind her with raffia fibers. They prickled her wrists and she stared back at his stony face with outrage. In his hands he held more of the raffia strands. He knelt between her forcibly parted legs, his knees pressing onto her thighs, immobilizing her to the floor. He twisted the fibers quickly in his hands until he had a short rope. She looked back at him, her dark eyes fearful but determined. She was a daughter of warriors, and she would not surrender.

Orpheo's fist rose, the rope trailing after it. He brought it down in a swishing crack onto one of her breasts. Vivian stiffened. It was like no pain she had ever felt. A stroke of lightning had appeared along her breast. She wanted to scream, high, long, fearful screams. Instead, seeing his passionate eyes above her, she ground her teeth together until she could hear them creak in her jaws. He raised his hand again and brought the lash down on the other breast. With an effort that brought tears to her eyes, and strained the cords of her neck, she raised her head to look at the results. He supported her neck with one hand. Two livid red marks ran lengthwise over each breast, barely missing the nipples. She sighed and sagged backwards onto a wooden block he had managed to place there. Now she could see the damage he wrought. He lashed her breasts again, and she sucked in air with a shudder. The lashes came now, fast and furious, each leaving behind a mark, and a streak of agony that did not have time to fade before the next one appeared. She heard a grunting, mewling sound, then realized that it came from her own mouth, and stopped it by an effort of will. By another effort she managed to open her tear-streaked eyes and to look into his. She was pleased to see a look of respect in her captor's otherwise immobile face.

The beating stopped. Her breasts and belly were marked by an elegant crisscross of marks. Her entire front burned. Suddenly she was conscious of the internal heat between her legs. Involuntarily her hips rose, and tried to force herself onto his body. He grasped her hips, as if readying her for penetration. His cock jutted out fully once again from the crisp curls at the base of his belly, and she could see the dangling heavy bag of his balls swinging between his legs. She smiled in anticipation, the burning hunger between her legs crying for satisfaction.

Orpheo twisted her hips suddenly, and Vivian found herself lying flat on the matting. This time, caught by surprise, she screamed. The fibers of the matting irritated her lashed breasts like thousands of tiny needles. He rose to stand above her, his calves constraining her torso. Her full buns were exposed to his gaze. Again he raised the fibers, bringing them down in a stroke against the fatty hemisphere. Beneath him, Vivian squealed, muffling her sounds in the flesh of her forearm. He lashed her again and again, ending with a single stroke down the length of her crack.

Vivian felt the first expected stroke on her ass as a counterpoint to the pain on her breasts. She shuddered and could not suppress a shriek. The second stroke brought no relief. Instead, the heat in the depths of her belly rose to a blaze she thought could go no higher until the next blow landed.

She was panting now, her legs spread wanting no more than something—anything would do—to assuage her need. Her cunt was a boiling mass of sensations, the smell, the touch of man would have sent her off into mewling pleasure. Her rational mind was aware of her condition, but so swept away in the tide of emotion that she could do, could be, nothing more than a demanding lust.

Orpheo, his cock enormous, poised at the entrance to her cunt, rose suddenly from her body. He took another strand of fibers from the table. This one was worked into a ring, tied in elaborate knots. He worked this rapidly over the knob of his maleness, making a collar at the tip of his cock. He knelt down between her legs, as her eyes watched hypnotized. His hands flashed forward once again, grasping one of her breasts. The coolness of his hands brought some relief to the weals on her pained flesh. With quick movements, he whipped some raffia around the prominent, aching nipple.

The grass fibers tied around her nipples raised the prominent flesh, cutting off sensation. Orpheo squeezed her breasts hard. The tip of his cock stirred against the entrance to her cunt. She screamed with frustration trying to trap the elusive member with her femininity, to suck it in. He avoided her easily, but the rough knots on the collar around his cock scraped painfully, dripping fire onto her bruised lower lips. Sensation cut off completely from her nipples. Then, with a flick of a half-seen blade, he opened the fetters and let her nipples loose. She screamed at the sudden agony as circulation returned, and he attached his mouth in demanding fierceness to the raised sensitive skin. She rolled her torso about, trying to loose him, but lost herself in the power of his movements. Then his cock stabbed deeply into her waiting cunt. She could not distinguish between the touch of flesh and the roughness of the fiber knots. Her insides were a churning mass of fire. Her whole body was on fire. His hands were over her, pulling her bruised ass to him, and she could feel his movements and the weight of his body on her. She screamed once more, this time in surrender and passion. Waves of pleasure raised her to peaks she had never experienced before. Her orgasm arced her body off the ground, supporting both of them on her heels and the crown of her head. She fell back on the matting, the prickling bringing about another earthquake in her system, and her legs went around his torso as she fainted amidst the sensations of pleasure and pain, with his own cock pumping life-fluid into her raging cunt.

He rose from her satiated body, heavy in a repairing doze. She rolled onto her elbows and knees and bowed as he passed by, saying the traditional words, "I am only your matting, chief."

Orpheo wrapped a lava-lava around his waist as he walked out. She heard the door come to as he stepped into the late afternoon sunshine.

She washed languidly, her hands full of clear water running under her breasts, exploring the bruises, then between her legs, reluctantly removing the exudations of his ferocious love-making. She winced slightly as she stroked the cuts, but the wince soon turned to pleasure as she recalled how each and every one was gotten.

He was standing under one of the palms looking out onto the tourists disporting themselves on Manahini beach. Bits of coral and pumice crunched pleasantly underfoot.

"They look so happy and carefree," he said, his voice a peculiar neutral tone. She had learned to watch that tone: it seemed always to precede action.

"And so rich," she said, laying a tentative hand on his arm.

He did not move, but his eyes followed the activities of a group of young Australians, bare-chested men and women, as they played a beach version of Australian football. The women's breasts bounced as they ran, amidst much giggling and screaming, particularly when there was a tackle.

Vivian saw the scene from his eyes, or tried to, and then she too licked hungry lips.

Orpheo saw the hunger in her eyes. "Is there anyone you would like?" he asked, indicating the cavorting people in the sand.

Vivian's eyes fixed on a small, very pale thin blonde whose small tits rode low on a prominent rib cage.

"She is so bony, so…unfeminine." Unconsciously she moved her broad shoulders and her loosely covered tits shifted enticingly. "But what would I do with her? I am a woman, not a man.…"

"Be a man for her."

The speed of her breathing increased, as the dark picture rose to her mind's eye. "Yes, yes," she breathed. And her tongue caressed her lips. Orpheo bent to kiss her, his tongue dipping deeply into her waiting moist mouth. "Tonight," he promised.

Chapter 4

The food was excellent. They ate sitting on the mat in the old style. Lime-cooked fish, baked taro, kava. He ate neatly, with precise bites, savoring every morsel. She ate hugely, enjoying her food, trying to emulate his quick neatness, failing and trying once again. He caught her eye and grinned. The grin was so boyish, so unexpected, she laughed heartily in return, and soon they were both rolling helplessly on the floor, ending with their faces close together, lying on the mat, wrapped in one anothers' arms.

"I will be back in a while," he promised suddenly, rose, and was gone. Vivian was in the middle of wondering whether and how she had offended him when his words came through the window at her head, "They will come to clear the things away. After that, open the wooden chest."

She looked again, and there was a key lying on the sill.

Her heart was beating rapidly when she raised the lid of the ornate Indian chest. Inside was another lid. Of some metal. The key fit and she raised the lid. A carved wooden mask glared at her, and she vaguely recognized a theme that she knew was current in another island. She lifted it reverently. Beneath was a woven belt, attached to it a curved phallus of black wood. Her breathing came in gasps, as she knew what to do. She stripped, laced on the woven straps of the mask, then the belt. The phallus was carved into a large hook at the bottom end, and she fitted that inexpertly into her own gaping hole. It rested snugly against her clitoris, grinding pleasantly into the wellsprings of her being. There was a small case of pigments as well, and she painted on her arm and breasts, in black and red, the traditional signs of warfare. Then, like any chieftain, she waited for her warriors to bring the victim.

Dorothy Fuller had long since ceased to resent herself. She was the runt of the litter, as her mother said, and she knew it. Now, peering into the dressing room mirror shortsightedly, she wondered at her daring in taking off her bra during the game in the afternoon. None of the men had paid the slightest attention to her, there being, as she knew, more attractive tits to look at.

In point of fact, she was technically still a virgin. She would happily have done away with the condition, but for her terminal shyness. The first occasion she had managed to entice the school stud into her bedroom, she had done so only to have him force her mouth down onto the broad thick head of his cock. At the touch of her willing yet fearful tongue, he had given a surprised yell, and a spurt of heavy hot, white liquid had inundated her lips and cheeks, some of the salty material running perforce down her throat. Her surprised cry had brought her father running.

One of her co-workers had shown an interest, and they had spent an evening petting heavily in the back of his car. He had removed her panties, and had mounted her quickly. Being as inexperienced as she, and she bent in the confines of the tiny Volkswagen, he had missed the mark, grunting joyfully to a climax in her tight and virginal ass. She had sobbed quietly, but been too shy to tell him the truth. He had avoided her later, for reasons she found unclear. And this trip, which was supposed to allow for romance, had been a disaster from the word go. Her fair skin had blistered, and she had had to stay out of the sun. The men weren't interested in her, since the revealing bikinis and the willingness of the other women had left her out of the running. And she hardly knew how to talk to the natives.

She stood at the window of her bungalow in one of Tau'tevu's tourist hotels, staring out to sea. It was pitch dark. She had read for a while in the hotel lobby, then watched the telly. Most of the others had been elderly vacationers, and though some of the men cast questioning glances at her, they were all too much under their assorted wives' eyes to do anything. There was a barely noticed gorgeous male, but he was there merely to buy something from the small shop, have a beer, and walk out, and the casual glance he cast in her direction was devoid of interest or emotion. So she had packed herself off to the room she shared with three other women from the office party. Now, dressed in an overlarge T-shirt proclaiming ironically TAU'TEVU—LOVE BENEATH THE PALMS, she stared blindly into the noisy dark.

The dark shadow blocked her view and caught her by surprise. A strong hand shot forward and seized her small breast painfully. She opened her mouth to scream and something, smelling sweetly of an herb she was unfamiliar with, was thrust into her mouth. Before she could react, befuddled by the fumes, she was hauled bodily through the large window and thrown onto a strong shoulder. The figure beneath her started running silently through the night, in the direction of the beach. She was conscious that she wore nothing under the shirt, and that he was holding her with on hand on her bare bottom. She started struggling, and he slapped her bare rump.

"Silence!" the figure said, her weight and his pace not making a noticeable difference to his breathing. "Be quiet."

Obediently, as she had all her life, Dorothy shut up before the male voice.

The door to the bungalow slid open. Vivian thought of switching on the lights. Instead, the mask on her head, she walked into the main room. Her lover was there. His head was encased in a smooth wooden mask, quite unlike her own. On the floor between his feet lay the body of the terrified blonde from the beach. Her large white T-shirt had been rucked up, displaying her in the gloom. An incongruously dark patch between her legs, she was staring wildly upwards, the whites of her eyes glinting in the faint light. Orpheo stood immobile above her. At Vivian's entrance his mask turned slowly to the bedroom door. Dorothy's eyes followed his and she let out a muffled gasp. There was a dark mass of something in her mouth, but her arms and legs were unconfined.

Vivian walked slowly, confidently, forward, the phallus swaying before her belly in counterpoint to the fluid movement of her tits. Its little hook, embedded between her nether lips, rubbed roughly against her inner recesses, and she almost cried out with the pleasure of it, with the anticipation. The blonde's eyes widened to frightened pleading rounds, and still Vivian came on. She squatted by the blonde woman's side.

Vivian's large brown palms seized the blonde's skinny knees and pulled them apart. Dorothy objected, writhing fearfully, the man's hand still on her mouth. She looked down her exposed body, past the small mounds made by her breasts, past the ridges of her ribs. The pale fluff of her pubic hair brushed high over her mound. Beyond that she saw the terrifying apparition of the large curved staff that stuck out from the woman's rounded brown belly. She screamed anew with fear of the awaited penetration. It would pierce and penetrate, but never sate the hidden fire she knew burned between her legs. She feared the penetration, the promise of pleasure that was never realized. Above the massive phallus swayed two full mounds of the woman's breasts. Dorothy's eyes locked helplessly on the two delicious rounds of flesh. They were tipped by darker protuberances, not pink as her own, but dark, almost black. Darker streaks crisscrossed them in a network pattern. Dorothy wanted to bite those protuberances, she suddenly realized, wanted to force them into the empty cavern of her body.

The woman leaned forward, from her kneeling position between Dorothy's thighs. Dorothy tensed, tried to cry out again. The woman threw herself on the skinny white body beneath her. The dong was an impediment, one she could have done without, for what she wanted now. She brought one full breast over the man's palm. Obligingly, he removed his hand and the gag from Dorothy's mouth and the breast plunged at the open, screaming mouth.

Dorothy found her lips silenced by the full mass of flesh she had, half-unconsciously, been waiting for. Her mouth clamped down on the mass of flesh. She felt the spongy roughness of the nipples, and the marvelous soft, buttery flesh of the full young breast. The woman's breast tasted salty, and Dorothy sucked hungrily at the musky taste, urging it in. In her frenzy she worried at the morsel with her tiny teeth, grunting contentedly. The mask above her screamed, and Dorothy, fearful of the worse, stopped biting. She returned to her senses, her watery blue eyes wide with fear. The mask, dark eyes glittering beneath the eye holes, stared back at her balefully. A strong hand raked the length of her side. Another grabbed one of her own small titties and squeezed with a power that brought tears to her eyes. Her jaws closed recklessly in a rictus of pain, and more of the full breast was shoved into her mouth.

It took a while for the wormy-fleshed woman beneath her to get the message, but finally Vivian found that her lusts were properly kindled. The young woman was unsparing with the use of her teeth, once she understood, by being hurt when she was wrong, that Vivian wanted her to use them. As she shifted her weight to pop first one, then the other breast into her captive's mouth, Vivian looked down. Long parallel scrape marks were plainly visible on the woman's thighs and chest. Her breasts, if such small nubbins in a grown woman could be called that, were flushed with strong red blotches around the aureoles, where she had been pinched unmercifully.

Vivian's hands drifted down between their sweating bodies to the juncture of their legs. The belly under hers rippled with tension. She parted the inner lips roughly, then thrust a long finger into the tight little opening. It was moist but still tight. The image of herself forcing her way into the tiny passage was irresistible. She tossed off her mask. Her hips rose, she grabbed the knob of the shaft, and doing so, worked the claw at the base of the rod roughly against her own clitoris. Dizzying, electrifying sensations followed. Her hips moved forward again, powered by her strong swimmer's thighs. The wooden rod penetrated deeply into the tiny orifice, the echoes of the tearing passage telegraphing thrills to Vivian's waiting clitoris. She shuddered deliciously, stretching herself out fully, with all her weight on the supine pale body beneath her. The skinny blonde's eyes rolled back in her head. She gave a low shriek as Vivian's weight came down upon her, then tried to bring enough air into her lungs against the weight to scream, but Vivian's demanding mouth, her teeth grinding against the blonde's lips, muffled the sound.

A feeling was beginning to build in Dorothy's body as the breasts, like full breadfruit waiting to be picked, were offered to her in turns. She was confused and frightened, but the mild pain she suffered was hiding a rising monster within her own frame. Unlike the time she had gone out with men, the fear was hiding a greater excitement, a feeling she had never had before and did not know how to handle. All she knew was that she wished this lovemaking, if that is what it was, would go on forever. But suddenly the fleshy morsel was pulled from between her teeth. She cried out instinctively, like a baby demanding the nipples. The woman above her, dark and menacing, but altogether promising, rose to her knees. She tossed off her mask with one hand, disclosing a dark and purposeful face, brown eyes glaring, full lips descending on Dorothy's own. The brown woman's other hand was between Dorothy's legs, exploring the folds roughly as any man. There was some more fumbling, and then Dorothy felt what she had feared all along. The knob distending her privates. For a second time stood still for her, then the mouth descended and the shaft forced itself inescapably into Dorothy's softest recesses. There was a brief, unfamiliar tearing sensation, then the hard intruder shouldered its way into the unexplored cavern, pushing aside the soft moist flesh. She screamed, but it was too late, the wonderful cruel mouth was exploring her own, biting and sucking, and her own was responding, in rhythm to the shrieking pain between her legs. Then the *kanak* woman was moving on top of her. The full breasts rubbed against her own. The hairless rounded belly, so unlike the two men she had previously been with, rubbed into her own bony frame like heavy cream. And the agony of having a foreign object inserted *there* was overshadowed, even blended, with the softness of the demanding frame that rollicked over her.

Vivian moved wildly, her mouth and hands, her artificial cock, her breasts, taking their pleasure of the supine captive beneath her. She screamed into the waiting mouth, and the blonde responded with muffled screams of her own. Vivian wanted more, she wanted to split the sacrificial body, to force her soul into that of the woman beneath her. Her powerful hips shuttled back and forth, ramming the artificial cock deeply into her prisoner's helpless body. She still wanted more. Her climax was approaching, and suddenly she knew what it was. She raised her head. Orpheo was a looming mass at the edge of her vision. His mask was still on. She turned pleading, demanding eyes on him. One of her hands moved around, pulling at a buttock, inviting him in, smoothing the entrance to her unoccupied rear hole. She knew with a rush of relief, accompanied by growing, demanding thrusts onto the passive unknown body beneath her, that he had understood. His hands parted her buttocks, and her speed increased. She could feel the heat from his thighs, the little hairs pricking at her buns, as he positioned himself. Beneath her, the pale face was twisted in a rictus compounded of pleasure and fear. Then his cock found its mark. To her surprise it was not the proffered rectal entrance that he chose. Instead his iron-hard cock found and pressed against her cunt, forcing the wooden spur deeper into the flesh of her sensitive clitoris. She screamed in earnest this time as he forced his way deeper and deeper into her demanding core. Then they both set to work, his movements amplifying hers, his hands gripping deeply into her full hips.

"Ahhhh," Vivian cried out her triumph. Then she looked down at Dorothy's pale twisted face and her teeth showed. "You will make a poor roast for the warriors, worm-flesh. The only thing you will be good for is pleasing me." She yanked painfully at Dorothy's pale head. "So do it properly, or I'll eat your cunt lips myself!"

The pleasure was now overwhelming Dorothy. The words she heard barely penetrated her thinking, and aroused savage pictures of cannibal feasts. And of the woman above her, with her face buried between pale thighs that she realized were her own. Involuntarily her legs rose in the air, her ankles seeking for purchase to hug the figure above her deeper into her. She felt the smooth sides of the woman, and above them the hairier ones of the man, wanted for a brief moment to resist, then realized that the man was interested not in her, but in the one who was fucking her. At that point she found herself slipping into nonsentience, her entire being involved in the pounding, tearing thrust of the body that held hers in thrall. A wave, barely noticed before, rose inside her mind. Pleasure engulfed her as it had never done before. The thrusts increased. Their speed and depth threatened to tear her apart. The *kanak* face above her was a demon mask, every muscle tense.

The two women screamed together into one another's mouths. Their hands became claws, raking one another's sides. Convulsions racked their insides, squeezing the wooden intruder, coating it with juices, running down their thighs. All three clutched at one another as the blinding light of orgasm shook the two women's frames. Orpheo tore himself from between Vivian's thighs. His cock was pulsing. Moving with all his usual grace and power, he knelt by the women's faces. His cock jetted a stream of white fluid which liberally inundated the women's faces. Dorothy wanted to turn her head, but the *kanak* woman above her extended a tongue, laving Dorothy's overheated face, spreading the sticky liquid over the hot skin. A final tremor racked Dorothy's frame, and she hungrily extended her lips for the other woman's offering.

Orpheo rocked back on his knees. The women, one brown, one pink, eyes closed, were lying cheek to cheek, their emotions and bodies spent. He rose leisurely, turned to take off his mask.

On the plane, Sydney-bound, Dorothy sat, rubbing herself meditatively. She caught the eyes of the stewardess on her. Unfathomable middle-aged eyes. For a second she stiffened in horror at having been observed, looking wildly around her to see if anyone else had noticed. All her fellow travelers were deeply asleep, and it was as if she and the uniformed middle-aged, anonymous woman were alone in the plane. Her movements became more deliberate, her hips arched, and a small smile played on her plain sunburned face. When she climaxed, she arched her body, knowing full well that she was being observed. The stewardess' impassive gaze was still upon her as she reached above Dorothy's head for the compartment, withdrew a blanket, and tucked it around Dorothy's drowsy body. Only the two of them knew that Dorothy's hand had dug deeply into the stewardesses full thigh, under her skirt, as she reached upwards. Or that the compliment was returned as the stewardess tucked the blanket around the passenger, while underneath it, for one brief moment, her fingers dug deeply into the sopping crotch.

Chapter 5

Hurrying through the shopping district, or what passed for it in Tau'tevu, Vivian stopped and frowned. The street was busy with people on their way to work, and tradesmen opening the doors of their shops. She wanted to give Orpheo something, something appropriate, perhaps something she herself could wear. One of Tau'tevu's only department stores...she would not have any time later.... Suddenly decisive, she strode into a shop entranceway covered with clothes hung on hooks. The store, as most on Tau'tevu, was run by an Indian immigrant. She could hear the lilting accent, almost Germanic, of his natal English as he discussed something with another customer.

"Can I help you?"

Vivian turned, startled. Huge black eyes, barely touched by eye-liner looked at her out of a perfectly oval face. The tiny red *tilak* mark between the brows highlighted the chocolate brown of the face, so different from her own deeper coloring.

"I'd like…," Vivian started to say. She stopped. In fact, she found with brutal self-discovery, that she was embarrassed. The saleswoman waited patiently. In an almost visionary flash, Vivian felt three things happening simultaneously. First, she felt, she would conquer this embarrassment. She was buying something for her man, and need fear no one's censure. Then, she realized as well, that she was completely indifferent to this woman's or any other person's opinion of her. Only one opinion mattered, and it was for that she was in the store. Finally, as she watched the patient face before her, she realized one more thing: this was what she had been looking for. Her eyes traveled the diminutive length of the woman with a demanding, almost insolent stare.

The salesclerk's long raven-colored hair hung in a braid to her waist. She was thin, thinner than most island women. Dressed as she was in a conservative skirt and blouse outfit, Vivian could not see what her figure was like, but her breasts bulged pleasingly inside the light yellow blouse, and though her calves were thin, they descended from generous hips. Suddenly Vivian realized that she had found what she had come for. A gift to please her lover and herself.

"I want a blouse," she said. "Transparent, something that will show my breasts, for my lover."

There was no reaction on the pretty face. The clerk turned on her heels and walked away into the depths of the shop. Vivian watched her go. There was a gliding sway to the receding figure that hinted at more than the armor of proper behavior could hide.

She returned almost immediately, her hands bearing several folded garments, and laid them on the counter. There were several blouses there, hideous things of semi-transparent polyester in vivid colors, and one was made of the fake macramé "art" that tourist women would buy with great giggles. Vivian looked at them, and without touching, raised her eyes to the clerk. The black eyes, in their large white orbs, looked back patiently, then dropped away.

"No." said Vivian, not even bothering to unfold the garments. She drew air into her chest, deeply, then turned to walk out, disdain in the very expansion of her nostrils.

"Wait!" the other woman called softly. Vivian kept walking. "Please?"

Vivian stopped and turned. There was a spark of something in the girl's eyes. "He is *very* special?" the Indian girl asked, almost in a whisper.

Vivian frowned, looking not unlike one of her violent ancestors deciding which prisoner to select as long pig. "Yes." she said finally. The clerk turned and hurried away. This time the sway was more pronounced, and there was less disdain in her eyes as she came back, holding a single package. She placed the paper on the counter and uncovered its contents. A simple blouse lay in there. It shimmered slightly. "Silk," she said succinctly. Vivian picked up the blouse and it flowed through her hands, almost crackling with a life and color of its own.

Vivian looked around. She and the girl seemed isolated in a bubble of time. A group of tourists haggling with an elderly salesclerk in another section were the only people visible. Deliberately, she undid her cotton blouse, took the silk and ran it over her exposed nipple. The dark, finger-like projection sprang to life. The salesgirl watched, her eyes wide, her lips together. Only a slight increase in the speed of her breathing indicated that she was aware of what Vivian was doing.

The touch of the silk on her bare sensitive flesh was electrifying. Shivers ran through Vivian's form. "I'll take it," she whispered hoarsely.

The woman named an almost outrageous price. Her voice was remote. She knew the *kanak*s would rarely spend sums of that sort on clothes. Instead, and to her obviously pleased surprise, Vivian simply produced the money from her handbag. Then, as the woman looked on silently, a faint look of puzzled pleasure in her deep eyes, Vivian dropped her cotton blouse completely. The clerk's eyes followed the line of Vivian's full breasts. There was approval, and something else in her glance. Her eyes traveled from one heavy, large-nippled breast to the other, not as if comparing them, but with a mixture of interested exploration and restrained emotion.

"You have been in an accident?" she asked. Her tone was low, not so much shy, as tentative, exploring, as if she wanted one answer, but expected another. Her eyes were on the crisscross marks on Vivian's breasts.

Vivian's eyes followed the other woman's gaze. "Not an accident. Certainly not an accident at all." She placed a slight emphasis on the word "accident."

She allowed the examination for a moment, then pulled on the other blouse. The silk was brisk and slick against her skin, and her nipples rose in full response. The clerk's breast was rising and falling noticeably now. Vivian looked at the other, then her hand, surrendering to an impulse, rose from the counter and placed itself squarely on the Indian woman's high breast. There was an immediate response. Not of withdrawal or outrage, but of thrust and pressure onto the palm laid flat on the hard mound. Tentatively, she raised her long fingered soft hand as well, and laid it on Vivian's nipple, which hardened more than ever.

"He must be a wonderful lover, for you to bring him gifts," the Indian girl said in a husky whisper. The tip of a pink tongue peeped out from her dark, almost bluish lips.

"Yes, and now I've found a gift to please him," Vivian said, her eyes firmly locked on the other's. "What's your name?"

"Padmini," she said. Vivian nodded once and turned away.

"I have a gift for you."

Orpheo smiled at her lazily, his hands still entangled in her frizzy hair. They were lying on the bungalow's matted floor. The fibers of the mats were scraping pleasantly into her back.

"You must approve, however," she said dreamily, pinching her own nipple that had risen at the tug on her scalp.

"You know I will approve," he said, but there was an alertness in his voice and a tenseness in his body, that had nothing to do with the action of his other hand, digging the tips of three fingers into the flesh of her breast.

"Still, you must," she panted, as the pain and lust rose in her groin. She wanted to force herself onto the pillar of his manstalk, but knew that it would not get her what she wanted, so she waited, trembling, for the next act. Knowing her needs better than she herself did, his palm flicked out and slapped the bruised breast repeatedly. Vivian groaned, her cunt flashing with moisture.

"Come, *vahine*, make me pleased."

She turned on him abruptly, like a tigress. "I am no commoner's plaything!!" she snarled at him. Her clawed hands raked at his exposed chest, once, then again. Long parallel scratches rose on his muscular belly. Orpheo barely reacted, his eyes hooded.

"I will return to my home!" She rolled over and scrambled to her knees.

The slick matting under foot hampered her move, and before she had made it onto her feet he was upon her. They crashed together to the floor, his weight driving the air from her lungs. Notwithstanding the weight of the body that now pinned her to the ground, Vivian fought on. Her breath came in gasps of effort. She struck backwards violently with one elbow and connected to an exposed rib cage. One of his hands was on her breast, pulling her to the mat, with the other he grabbed her hand and twisted her arm high above her back. She could feel his teeth clamp on the muscles of her shoulder. Vivian bared her own teeth ferociously. As she struggled his hand abandoned her bruised breast while his weight continued pushing her into the matting. She knew what was to come and crossed her ankles, hoping to keep the expected invasion of her inner recesses at bay. When he raised his weight slightly to allow his hand access between their bodies she bucked suddenly, almost succeeding in throwing him off. She tried to roll over again, but the grip on her arm stopped that maneuver. His hard hand descended painfully and delightfully on her full buttock. His knee was against her thighs, pushing them powerfully apart. The hand snaked into the available crack and reached for her moisture. She squealed sub-vocally as he found his mark. This time he took no chances. Powerful fingers hooked into her moistened hole. The distention was painful, almost as painful as a dry fuck would have been. Vivian struggled more, hoping the effort and friction would increase the luster of feelings she was already experiencing. He forced a third finger into the recesses of her cunt, and then his heavy muscular hips followed the pull of gravity and descended between her spread thighs, limiting her options severely. She started moaning in time to her low ragged breathing.

Vivian felt the masculine intruder push against the bruised lips of her cunt. He thrust hard. The long thick shaft spread the walls of her vaginal channel. She screamed, once, briefly, when she was properly breached. It was a scream of both surrender and triumph. Orpheo pulled out almost to the end, and Vivian collapsed forward on the mat. Supported only by her shoulder, her other hand reached back and raked his flank mercilessly. He thrust hard into her in response, battering his hips and belly against her bruised behind. He started a driving rhythm which sent shivers up her body with each thrust. She clawed at him unmercifully with her free hand every time he withdrew.

When the waves of pleasure seemed almost unbearable, when she felt the top of her skull about to explode, and the discomfort of her position was so mixed with pleasure that she did not know where one sensation started and the other ended, he climaxed. Gushes of warm sperm inundated her insides. His cock pulsed with a life of its own, and his face, which she could see over her shoulder from the corner of her eyes, twisted in a rictus of pleasure.

The idea that he was taking his pleasure from her helpless body, that he was simply enjoying her proved a final stimulus. Vivian's cunt pulsed, her insides contracted and she gave a long wail of satisfied lust as wave after wave of pleasure washed through her body.

They lay joined on the matting, for a long time while trickles of their merged exudations made their way from the joining of their flesh through the forest of her hairs to drip on the mat in fat globules. At last Orpheo rolled off her.

She smiled into his glowing face. "Now you'll go and look at my present. It's not something you can just pick up, or buy...." She smiled mischievously.

Orpheo walked into the shop with his usual arrogant, unhurried stride. He looked without expression at the trinkets and cheap clothing, stopping only to admire a tapestry hanging on one of the walls. The owner, an elderly Indian gentleman, watched quietly from one of the counters. Orpheo picked up some minor purchases, then drifted over to the women's clothing section. A dark, slight girl was watching his progress with the dull eyes of the experienced salesperson who knows a window shopper when she sees one.

Padmini gazed at the browser out of the corner of her eye. She could not tell where he was from, or what

Tau'tevu

he was. He had the bronze darkness that might have marked him an Indian but for the pale hair. His features were too sharply chiseled, his look arrogant. It was his voice, though, his voice and the movements of his hands as he examined the fabrics she brought to him. She trembled as she heard him speak, wanting him to go on and on, knowing that anything that voice commanded her she would do. And yet, he barely looked at her. Her pink tongue touched her lips nervously. Nervous from his proximity and her own boldness, as well as for the consequences if her family discovered she was...attracted...to someone not of her caste or people.

In the evening she lay on her bed in the hot tiny room at home. Around her was the rustle of the house. The sound of her mother saying something to her father. Radh, her brother, moving about after a shower, singing a popular song. The image of his dark torso came to mind and sent a shiver down her stomach. Restless, she turned on the light, peered about. She rose and looked at herself in the mirror, slipping off her thin nightgown.

Staring back at her was a dark girl, too dark to be wholly fashionable. On her forearm was the whitish pigment-less patch that was the cause of her anguish and grief, and of her unmarried state. There was another, a tinier one under one rounded breast. She touched the dark, almost black nipple, and it sprang erect, almost the length of the first joint of her little finger. Her ribs were showing under the arch of her breast, but the round of her belly was firm, with a deep dimple at her navel. Between her thighs stood the perfect female triangle, darker than the rest of her skin, completely hairless. At the point of the triangle peeped her full soft lips, hiding the inner folds so innocently. She looked at herself critically. Her calves were a trifle too thin, her haunches a trifle too full for perfect beauty, but the rest of her would have excited the interest of a prince. She turned to show her back and behind. Black luminous eyes in a heart-shaped face peered back at her like fathomless wells. Her back was straight and perfect, unmarred. Her waist squeezed her torso into the size a man (well, she admitted honestly, a large man, a man with large, strong, voracious hands, like the Anglo in the shop today) could hold with both hands. And below them swelled taut, almost boyish buttocks, dark as the rest of her, bisected by a perfect line.

Her hand stole down her back, to the crack of her ass. The other hand joined, and she parted her buns, looking at the smooth skin around her anal port. She touched it, still moist and clean from her nightly bath, and shuddered at the caress.

Her breathing was coming quickly now, mixed with frustration and anger. She threw herself on the bed, then reached for the drawer of her night table. It was usually locked, and she had installed the lock herself. Her mother would not have approved, had she known, that her daughter was such an expert handywoman. She would have approved even less of the contents of the drawer, though, Padmini considered, perhaps not. Her mother still thought of herself as a traditionalist, preserving Indian culture, and this, undoubtedly, was a part of it. She took the book in hand and tried to read the Hindi, stopped in frustration, and read the English translation on the opposite page.

Tau'tevu

Lying flat on her stomach, her legs parted without a thought. Padmini's hand stole under her belly, caressing the slickness at the lowest point of the dome as she read Vatsyayana's words. As always, she teased herself with reading the less interesting parts first. Her slender brown fingers, unbidden, touched the top of her slit, then slid inside to stroke the already-erect button. She pushed down hard against the firm touch and was rewarded with a thrill of pleasure. Gradually, as she sank into the book, her stroking became harsher. Her tight buttocks pushed deeper into her hand until, with a cry of frustration, she began tearing at her lips, pinching them roughly. Then she turned to the chapter she favored, examining the many ways of pleasure a man could find in a woman obedient to his demands. The chapter on bites brought about gasps of pleasure which she found she could not control as with one hand she pinched her inner lips, and with the other, her erect nipples. It was the seventh chapter that forced her to hide her face in her pillow and bite her lip. Hastily she reached into the drawer again and extracted the Japanese *mano-no-te* that she had brought from the shop. It was of hard wood, in the shape of a small hand attached to a long handle. The butt was a round cup enclosing a rubber ball. She raked her flanks with the clawing wooden hand, and when her climax approached, struck her buttocks hard with the ball, her eyes glued to the page.

She caught sight of herself in the mirror. As if mesmerized, she rose and posed before the reflection. Her hand rose and she brought the stick down against her rounded belly with a splat. She controlled her gasp at the sudden pain, but her belly fluttered. Behind the fluttering, between her legs, she felt a glow begin. Hastily, fearful of being discovered, she raked the tool against her belly, her breasts, her buttocks. It was insufficient, she knew. Throwing the stick aside, she parted her legs and stuck her hips wantonly forward. Opening the dark, almost black lips, she grasped the squishy flesh with her fingers and started rubbing furiously, her eyes closed.

There was an intake of breath behind her. She turned in dismay, her hand flashing, moistly, from between her legs. Radh was standing there. His eyes were large, luminous, his hands clenched and unclenched aimlessly. His mouth was slightly open, and a ringlet of dark hair fell over his eyes, still damp from the bath. There was no doubt he had been watching her for some time. The front of his white *dhoti* bulged forward, and he was panting. With what grace she could muster she stalked over to the bed and pulled her nightdress to her. She smelt the perfume of herself on her fingers, and, for an instant, her eyes closed languidly and she drew the smell in, still holding the fabric. Radh took one step toward her, but when she turned to watch him, knowing she would not stop him, he gave a strangled cry, looked at her naked form one last moment, then fled.

Padmini flung herself down on the bed again. It was moist with her exudations. There were tears in her eyes as she rubbed furiously at her waiting mound. The climax finally overtook her. Her insides erupted as a volcano: hot and gushing and she rolled onto the shaft of the instrument, bruising and crushing her *yoni* against the wood, praying for the future. At last, after hiding her instruments, she fell into a troubled sleep in which a magnificent man, about to seize her with powerful hands, dissolved suddenly into the thin air of her vision.

The hut on Taulea Point was lit by the last orangey colors of daylight. Orpheo stood in the middle, proudly erect, a short length of white fiber in his hand. As Vivian approached and knelt before him, he roped the wet fibers around his member. The head glowed a brighter red, and flesh bulged through the spaces between the ties. She started panting, enthralled by the sight and by the tiny transparent drop of fluid that had appeared at the hungry tip. Obedient to his commanding look, she dropped her clothes, her shoulders moving her heavy breasts provocatively. Orpheo strode over to her. His hands enmeshed in her plentiful wiry hair, he gazed deeply into her eyes, then bent and kissed her passionately, his tongue exploring her mouth savagely. His erection in its cage of fibers rubbed against her belly and she moved herself closer, to enjoy more of the rough contact. Then he reached behind him. In his hand was a mass of combed and beaten coconut fiber. He swiped the bundle over her breasts. It prickled pleasantly, and Vivian moved with the sensation. Then he grabbed her breast and twisted it hard around. He stopped for a second, his fathomless dark eyes regarding her for a moment, as if expecting something. She puzzled for a moment, then began to struggle wordlessly, trying to extricate her mammary from his fiber-roughened hand. He let her go abruptly, and the sudden release sent her flat on her back, her breast tingling. Orpheo was on her in a flash. She struggled wordlessly, raking her hands at him. He caught her wrist in an inflexible hand. His other rose, and the bundle came onto her back, leaving a patch of burning across the skin. He pulled her wrists down to the mat-covered floor. The first shock of the fibers against her jiggling buttocks was barely tolerable. The second stroke flashed against her skin just as the aftershock of the first blow began tingling her buttocks. Vivian shrieked briefly, her behind shuddering. His hand dropped from her hair.

"Stay there!" he ordered.

Vivian crouched before him. Her brown full moons pointed to the roof of the hut. Her back was sleek and supple, muscles playing enticingly beneath the skin. She had the broad shoulders of the experienced swimmer and her spine arched, covered by smooth skin. For a brief second Orpheo admired the scene. His face emotionless, he struck again at the upthrust bottom. Vivian hissed an in-drawn breath but did not move, except for a quiver that ran through the fatty part of her upthrust buns. He struck again, raising a tangle of welts on the perfect skin. His hand rose and fell like a metronome, and with each lash her behind reddened, blooming through the brown cover. Tears coursed down her cheeks, but she clenched her jaws and persevered while her behind ran with fire and agony traced its way up her spine.

When Vivian felt she could take no more, when the agony in her ass was overpowering, he struck a final blow and stood still. Sweat was dripping from his forehead and slicking his shoulders. He knelt by her side and ran a palm over the lacerated skin, pebbled with the marks of his strokes. The touch of his rough-skinned palm shot a spasm of sensation up Vivian's spine. She was his now, his to do with as he wanted. Her insides were like jelly, completely subservient to any whim he might express. It was no surprise when he knelt behind her, and without any preamble, stuck four stiffened fingers deep into her waiting vagina. The fingers slipped inside to the last knuckle and Vivian bent her head once more in acceptance and joy. He yanked his fingers out and she waited expectantly for the thrust of the fiber-covered member that was to come. She knew the coir fibers would tear and lacerate her insides as they had her bum. Instead he shoved the same cone of fingers into her rectum. At first the strong ring muscles resented the intrusion and fought the invader, then she forced herself to relax, forced herself to accept his anal penetration, impersonal and invasive as it was.

He bent over her "No proper *vahine* would accept all that!" The contempt in his voice, its utter sneering quality, galvanized her into sudden action. Suddenly she knew what was missing in her pose of surrender. She bucked against him suddenly, throwing him to the floor, turning on him with fingernails backed by strong swimmer's fingers, and with healthy teeth. He cuffed her head from side to side. Dazed, she still tried to reach him, growling incoherently the while. He grabbed her flailing hands, bending them behind her back. And when she tried to bite his shoulder, he slammed her cheek away with a hard shoulder. Twisting, he held both her hands behind her back. Teeth clenched, Vivian fought back.

Orpheo threw her onto the polished log bench. His knee in the middle of her back, he seized one ankle, bringing it up to her haunch. She started struggling, and he persisted in his activities, looping some of the softened coir around her ankle and then roping it tightly to her thigh. She screamed loudly and he paid no attention, though when she flailed at him he grasped both her wrists and tied them together behind her neck. Before she knew how to react she found a rope loop around her waist. She tried to roll off onto the floor, but his weight was upon her, crushing her to the smooth bench.

When it was over Vivian was panting, trying to suppress her agony. Her ankles had been tied tightly to the backs of her thighs. Wrists together behind her back were tied by a length of coir to a loop that ran round her waist. Her mouth was held open by a wooden ring tied in place. The coir fibers bit into her skin and every time she tried to improve her position by moving about, she found a new pain.

Orpheo stepped away from Vivian. The backs of his hands were scratched where she had managed to reach him with her nails. She watched him, then made a fright mask of her face, squinting eyes and protruding tongue like the curse masks of the old religion.

He pulled her head back by her hair until the tendons in her neck protested, then moved forward. She could feel the salty-sweet taste of his fluids, heavy on her tongue, but could not bite due to the ring. She tried to eject his member with her tongue, but the force behind his rod was more powerful, and he drove into her, raping her mouth.

She mumbled curses around the obstruction in her mouth. Involuntary tears came to her eyes, but they were tears of pain and anger, not frustration nor weakness. The pulsing in his member warned her and she tried to pull back, but was held fast by his fingers around her jaws. Suddenly her mouth was full of spurts of salty-acrid cream as he flooded her mouth with his offerings. Again she tried to pull away, to give herself time to swallow and breath but his iron grip held her fast. Rivulets of come dribbled down her chin, pooling on the bench and she could smell the musty unmistakable scent of male lust.

She though he would stop, instead he rolled her over. She looked up at the pole and straw thatching and tried to move. He was between her knees, pulling her legs apart. Then the thrust of his wrapped cock came up her vaginal channel.

This time Vivian screamed in earnest. The sensation was an incredible mixture of scraping pain and a pleasure that lit off every nerve end in her quim. Now she knew why the old chieftains had wrapped their cocks with fiber before deflowering a captive. The sensation was unforgettable, she knew. She screamed again, a long ululating call, as Orpheo set to work to fuck her. The thrust of his shaft up her softened insides was a saw that abraded the nerves to the back of her skull. The climax grew from some primitive part of her that wanted only more and more sensation. She climaxed first, unable to control her movements because of the rope, crying in frustration. He rose over her. Something glittered that came down swiftly in a terrible arc. Then her limbs were free, cut from the coir by the knife, and he was spilling some more of his male liquor into her receptacle. She arched her body once, weakly, then tried to clutch her lover by the strength of her thighs and knees. The pulsing of her insides shook her entire body, and as her senses drained away from her, she was aware that her body, completely out of control, was shaking with the power of orgasm.

She came to as his hands, dripping with oil, rubbed smoothly over her hurting limbs. She sighed luxuriously and stretched, though every movement brought a twinge of pain. Smiling languidly, the pain causing her to recall the pleasure, she stretched again.

Chapter 6

Padmini walked on the boardwalk, skillfully avoiding passersby. Before her a hire-car—one of the large American ones owned by an Anglo company—slowed to a stop. As she came opposite it the front door opened, blocking her path. Startled, she looked down. He was there, holding the door open. Looking up at her. The *kanak* girl was driving, looking straight ahead. Padmini's heart started pounding in her chest. She licked her lips nervously. The man who had stepped out of the car looked on, without a word. His full lips were slightly parted, and a quizzical look was in his eyes. Padmini made a move to step to one side. He anticipated her action, and then shrugged slightly. A gesture of disappointment, from a man not used to them, but philosophically ready to accept them. There was also something else in his expression—contempt, perhaps. She bent and stepped into the car. He slid over, his hand helping her, and somehow, without him having gotten out, she found herself ensconced between the driver and the man. The girl did not even look at her, as the car started off through the raucous traffic of pedicabs, elderly sedans, and donkey carts.

They drove in silence to the outskirts of the "city" of Tau'tevu, then down a dirt track between hedges towards the sea. This was an area Padmini had never been in before, even though it was close to her family's house: it was *kanak* area, and Indians were not welcome. Through a break in one of the hedges, around a thicket of pandanus hung with *kava* plants, they found themselves before a large native-style thatched house. The *kanak* woman left the keys in the car and stepped out, as did the man. They stood away from the car and waited for Padmini to follow, and now she knew it was her own decision to make. She could restart the car and drive away. Or.... She watched the two backs disappear into the hut.

The hut was large, divided into several rooms: unusual in a native house. The entrance was a typical *kanak* place, furnished with well-woven mats and carved wooden chests. She walked through a hanging into another room. This one was hung with rich fabrics. A large chest of Chinese manufacture, replete with brass fittings stood in one corner. Next to it, incongruously, a suit of armor of oriental appearance. There was a magnificent Mughal portrait on the wall, and a book bound in leather and unfaceted jewels rested on a mahogany lectern. Dominating the room, however, was a large bed. Its posts were carved dark wood, and the bedspread was of silk dyed to a Rajput design. The man was there, sitting on the bed and leaning against a bolster. The *kanak* woman stood beside the bed, her hand possessively on the man's ankle. Padmini walked slowly forward, her hips swaying heavily to barely heard *vina* music from hidden speakers.

Orpheo lay back on the bed and merely looked at Padmini. Vivian stared at the Indian girl with curiosity and some hostility, then deliberately started taking off her clothes while the other two watched. She made a production of it. First the newly-bought silk blouse. Then she stroked her full brown breasts, slid her hands over her full stomach, then deeper under the waistband of her skirt. She pushed it down, until the curly tips of her pubic fleece showed, then let it fall. She wore no underclothing, and displayed her fine strong body with evident pleasure. Padmini noted with approval the stripes and bruises on the softer parts of the woman's flesh. She smiled faintly. This...all this...seemed to be what she had waited for.

The man rose and stood by the bed. The *kanak* woman took off his jacket and undid his tie, then dropped the fine linen and the silk on the floor carelessly. His shirt followed, then she knelt to undo his pants. The man's hand rested comfortingly on the kneeling woman's head. When some clumsy move of hers discomforted him he simply twisted the mass of hair in his fist and jerked her neck sharply. Padmini smiled in gratification and approval: this was the way one dealt with slaves.

Finally he stood before her. His body was subtly muscled, and not at all subtly aroused. It was the first time Padmini had ever seen what she had only dreamt about. She examined it covertly, then when she noticed the amused expression of the *kanak* concubine, looked fully at the engorged staff. She reached for her hair pins and let her jet-black hair drop.

Padmini's heart was pounding. In some ways she was a very old-fashioned girl. While her friends, at the college and at home were reading modern romances and dreaming of Indian movie stars, she herself was reading the old romances and sagas. Her parents approved—such a well-bred girl, so interested in our culture—but would have approved less if they could see her daydreams. The vision of princes in their harems, magnificent in their jewelry, and she, the head of the harem, commanding and being commanded. Now it was like that. She looked around. The bungalow room had been decorated with the opulence of the truly rich: those who do not care to make an impression.

Her hands went behind her to undo the buttons of her bodice. She let it fall to the floor. The slaves would pick it up. Her prince watched with expressionless eyes. I will change it for you, my prince. I will change your expression to that of the tiger, she thought. She swayed in the movements of a dance only she could hear, but was not surprised to notice the growing tapping of a *tabla* as she swayed. Her bra was plain cotton. Her hands caressed her own back for a fraction, then the constricting thing fell at her feet. The beat speeded up. Her feet pounded on the carpets of the floor, almost, but not quite, soundlessly.

The man made a slight movement with his fingers. The slave, ever vigilant to his needs, hurried to produce a silk-covered case. Her eyes fully on him, Padmini saw him open the case. The first item he produced was a thin, flexible shaft of spotted bamboo. It had been taken from the root end, and the nodules, prominent and gnarled, were set close together. Padmini's tongue fluttered against the inside of her lip at the sight, and her belly felt hollow. He reached into the case again and procured another springy shaft. This one ended in a curious head which looked like a group of fingers pinched together, and yet bore the features of a fierce bird of prey, including an upturned ruff which flared like a miniature peacock's tail behind the bird-like head. Finally he produced a black, long lashed whip. The lash was a thin, shiny trail that dropped from his fingers like the coils of a snake.

It would be the lash, she knew. The lash would be first. Padmini, still dancing, closed her eyes, twirled her body. Then she realized that would seem like she was afraid, and she slowly opened her large almond eyes to the light of the room. Her hips still moved in the dance, and her hands, but her body was still, waiting. And her eyes never left her prince.

He raised the lash slowly, then when his hand was extended over his head, he sent the instrument flicking through the air. It curled around her, from right to left, stroking her from right hip, over her buttocks, to left hip, with the tip ending at the base of her belly, just above the darker skin where she conscientiously shaved every couple of days.

The world came to a stop. A burning line of fire had sprouted across her ass, and a blow, like nothing she had ever felt before, struck her middle. She bravely contained the scream that was about to erupt from her mouth, as her shuddering body contained the pain, the sudden excitement, the pleasure that rose like a wash of hot air from her loins. A haze rose in her vision, though she managed to keep her eyes still. She looked at her prince's face and realized that there was a faint look of disapproval on the aquiline brow. Then she recalled the book, and a blush of faint shame rose from her belly to her face. She knew that next blow she would do better. He raised the whip again, and brought it flicking down. This time the tip of the lash barely flicked her black nipple, like a naughty boy flicking a fly with his fingers. This time Padmini was ready. The pain was very mild, a game, a teaser. The cry she made was appropriate, her "Ay!" loud, but not too loud. He smiled in gratification. The slave squatting beside him, his member in her hand, smiled in contempt. Padmini's dancing smile changed not a bit. The bitch was an uncivilized one, what did she know?

The prince flicked the lash at her. His movements were painful, intended to embarrass and trick rather than punish. Once, twice over her shoulder, and she cried out. Again, teasingly, over one hip, then a couple of quick flicks at her feet.

The heat in her body rose, searched for the contact. Padmini could feel the familiar heat press against her from between her legs. Her skin was burning now, even though these were mere childish pranks, and she laughed aloud, through the dance, at the sensation. The music was winding down and he took aim one last time. The lash flicked out, straight to its target. The tip flicked once, at the top of the smooth dark, almost black crack at the base of her perfect belly. The nub of sensitive flesh she had touched, pinched, hurt so many times was there, waiting, confident. This small lash, however, was nothing like the love pats she had given her clitoris before. Padmini gasped with the pain that rocked her from the base of her spine to the top of her head. Then she gave out, involuntarily, an unfeigned cry, a scream, cut off by sheer force of will.

Padmini stood, frozen in the last figure of the dance, her hand extended gracefully above her head, one foot firmly on the ground, the other raised. The man looked at her for a long burning moment, his gaze traveling the length of her body. The slave's head was bobbing up and down on his lap, and Padmini could see, without focusing on the scene, the length of shaft that rose from the curls at the base of his belly. She wished fleetingly that men would shave as well, to display themselves more fully.

"Display your beauties!" he commanded roughly.

Padmini's heart melted at the order. She sank gracefully to the carpeted floor. Rolling over, she arched her back to expose her rounded behind. She knew how enticing the full moons of her ass, pierced by the long crack would be. Then she rose and stood on one leg, extending a foot high and to the side, exposing the length of her crack. She raised her breasts to his view, then sank down again on her heels, and spread her knees. Her body arched backwards until her shoulders touched the floor and her cunt was a gaping pink slash in the dark skin of her mound.

"Come here!" he whispered.

Padmini rose and swayed towards the bed, her eyes enormous. She lay down on the bed. He indicated what he wanted with a touch of his fingers. Her feet rose and crossed behind her neck. Her arms went behind her, each hand seizing the opposite elbow. She looked down over her breasts, the folded belly, the prominent cunt to where his face looked broodingly into hers. Then he raised his hand.

Vivian watched the Indian girl display herself. She was as flexible and quick as an eel, the *kanak* thought. The shaven cunt she found both attractive and repellent, its dark, almost gray surface distracted from the pure beauty of the lips, the tiny slit. Vivian wanted to run her mouth, no, her teeth, along that perfect shape, to tear and nip at it. Orpheo's hand pushed at her head urgently now, and she took in the whole of his long cock. Tears broke out in her eyes as she fought her gag reflex, and then the knob was in her throat and she had learned, almost miraculously, to breath without disturbing it. Something like swimming she realized, while her head went up and down to the sound of the muffled pounding feet and the eerie Indian dance music.

Orpheo released her head and pulled her upwards. The dance was over and the Indian girl was posing again. She was exquisite, and notwithstanding her distaste for Indians in general, Vivian was entranced. Orpheo ordered the girl onto the bed, and she lay there, contorting herself into an impossible knot which exposed her femininity to his avid gaze, and to the assault of anything he wished.

The blow came not from his hand, but from the side where the concubine had been sitting unnoticed. The knotted bamboo whistled through the air and struck bruising flat against the fully prominent ass, wielded in a quiet ferocity by the *kanak*.

"Pah!" Padmini shouted in an explosive release of air. The blow had shaken her to the core, but she saw her prince's eyes upon her and realized there should be no reaction to the slave's presumption, because it was no presumption at all. She was being beaten by her master, merely using another device. The bamboo rose again, came down parallel to the first. The bamboo joints drew agony into her skin, and with it, a rise of heat in her exposed *yoni*.

The man's eyes glowed and Padmini followed his avid gaze once more to the softness of her own body, to the quivering of her taut belly. Lines of fire were etching themselves with each blow on her thighs, and tears were spurting in her eyes. Suddenly he bent forward and applied his mouth to her belly. The touch of his lips and tongue brought a coolness to the cruel heat generated by the savage blows that striped her spread thighs. She shivered again, this time with a combination of dread and pleasure, the pain receded, framed the lust she was feeling. Then his movements grew stiffer and he launched himself upon the upper half of her torso. His hands grabbed fistfuls of her breasts, mauling them in cadence with the lashes on her thighs. His cruel mouth descended on her black nipples, pulled into tiny peaks, pinpoints of pain, by the pressure of his hands. He sucked them into his mouth and Padmini cried out in an agony of pleasure as first his tongue then his cruel teeth scraped against the sensitized little buds. His mouth roved higher, biting the tops of her breasts, then laving her neck and the bottom of her jaw with exquisite passion. He stared fiercely into her eyes for a brief second, then his lips clamped to hers. She fought against the lingual invasion to no avail, and his tongue forced its way past her bright white teeth and into the welcoming warm cavern of her mouth. In surrender she allowed him to explore her, to rape the innocence of her mouth with his own.

The blows on her thighs, a rain of fire she had been conscious of throughout his assault on her mouth ceased, and suddenly there was another mouth, *there* preparing her for his invasion. She felt with her right hand. His enormous cock was lying beside her, and she worshipped it with her hand, fondling the glans, rubbing the sticky secretion into the shaft and head, her long fingers helping her visualize what the fleshy monster would do to her insides. Panting, he raised his head from her, and Padmini knew a moment of fear. The look in his eyes was infinitely cruel and lustful, the eyes of a true master, and she knew she was no more than a passive mote in his eyes. Then the marvelous lips withdrew from their exploration of her lower caverns where a glow had started, flowing over the cuts on her thighs. The *kanak* slave was there, by her side, her face shiny with Padmini's juices. The *kanak* manipulated their master's body with her hand. The man looked at her exultantly, and Padmini knew what she had to do. She held onto the shaft, then guided it inexpertly, fumbling until she found the disgustingly hairy crack of the woman's fat outer lips. With a cry, her prince surged forward into the concubine's waiting orifice, and Padmini could feel the fat lips parting to the brutal assault.

Orpheo's cry was echoed by Vivian as he forced his way into her channel in a sudden surge. He cried out again, a long "Aaaagh" of passion before his mouth and hands descended once again onto the Indian woman's body. He mauled the dark breasts, pinching the nipples again and again, then lowered his face and started licking the woman's body with a rough tongue. He stopped long enough to thrust his tongue deeply into the broad mouth. Padmini's eyes were shining and she scratched incessantly at the man above her. His hips kept on thrusting deeply into Vivian's recess, his massive organ thrusting deeply into her bringing with each thrust a wave of pleasure.

Vivian watched as Orpheo started striking the Indian girl. He bunched his fingers together and struck her several times on her breasts, then using only his thumb he dug into her rib cage. Padmini's thin frame quivered with pain though her hips shook with pleasure. Orpheo's movements in Vivian's cunt speeded up until the continued slap of his belly against hers, merged with the slaps of his hands on Padmini's skin to become almost a continuous sound. Vivian felt the rise of his tension as his cock jerked and ground into her. Padmini, lost in a world of her own, was approaching her own climax. Her controlled artificial-sounding yelps had turned to yowls of mixed pain and pleasure. Then finally Orpheo ground himself viciously into Vivian's welcoming thighs. His cock erupted in a flood of soothing liquid that splashed against her insides and overflowed over her inner thighs and onto the silk bedcover. Padmini cried out once more, a wordless scream of pleasure and anguish. Her insides flooded with salty liquid and seemed to melt. Vivian, feeling the pleasure of the two bodies she was assisting, convulsed as well, and her arms and legs clutched Orpheo's muscular body to her own. She turned her head in her pleasure only to meet Padmini's almost eyeless stare. Without thought her mouth opened and she kissed the Indian girl deeply, their tongues meeting in pleasure for the first time.

Above them the palm trees on Taulea Point whispered softly in the never-ending winds, and inside the hut they carried the smell of pandanus and of lust well satisfied.

Orpheo rose from the bed, and the two women looked at his muscular backside while he rummaged on a low table. Padmini gradually loosened the muscles that had cramped in her wild lustful last moments. Vivian's arm was across her chest, one large hand playing idly with a small black nipple. Her own hands, she was surprised to find, were exploring the *kanak* girl's cunt.

"I am Padmini," she said shyly, her face returning to its normal almost passive look.

"I know," the large *kanak* woman smiled at her, then kissed her gently once, then again, fiercely and demandingly. "I'm Vivian. And you, princess, are very beautiful."

Padmini shook her head slightly, shyly, then raised her lips to be kissed again. She stopped when she saw Orpheo looming impassively above the bed. He held a decorated mirror in his hand. She looked at him in puzzlement.

"Look!" he commanded, bending forward and spreading her legs. Vivian, resting on one elbow, divined his intention, and pulled an embroidered bolster beneath the slimmer woman's head. Padmini looked down the length of her body at the reflection of her naked cunt. It was framed by angry red stripes that crossed the perfect framing hemispheres. The tiny droplets of blood from the beating had dried, but the red gave evidence of the severity of her sensations. The man parted the lips showing the coral-pink inner recesses. The deep inner hole was still obscured by the fine membrane of her virginity. He let her look at herself for a moment, then his finger moved until it was touching and barely penetrating the tight clenched star-like entrance of her rear portal. She shivered at the touch, knowing that that entrance too was intended for his pleasure. And hers. For a brief second his head dropped and she felt his tongue lave the length of her crack, from her tailbone to the hood that hid her clitoris, then his tongue was withdrawn. Suddenly she realized what he had given her: the chance to be deflowered twice, once when she had mentally become a woman, next time when he would physically penetrate her. Orpheo's face transformed when he saw the realization touch her, and a final shudder shake her body.

"Tomorrow," he whispered with a smile.

Chapter 7

Padmini waited until the bustle of the household had died down. Her hand was between her legs, fondling the newly created opening, pleasing herself in the wetness and the slightly raw feeling. Every time she touched herself she could feel a shiver run through her frame. She gasped at her own touch, twisting in the sheets until they wrapped themselves around her brown limbs.

She rose when the power of her desire threatened to overwhelm her. There was a dark blue sari in the closet. Padmini wrapped it around herself without bothering with underclothes or a blouse. She slipped out of the house and hurried through the dimly lit streets. There was a guitar playing somewhere in the dark of the night, and from another house she could hear the soulful tones of a popular Filipino band.

The house on Taulea Point seemed completely dark until one noticed the tiny glow near the entrance. It was caused by a calabash filled with tiny glowing fireflies, and barely lit the steps up to the porch. Padmini laughed with childish glee at the beauty of the insects, and stepped quietly into the hut. The first two rooms were dark, but she knew where she was going, and parted the heavy hangings with a trembling hand. They were waiting for her, her prince and the slave. The bracelets on her wrist clinked together, and she glided into the room.

He was on the bed, completely naked, his phallus jutting out before him. The *kanak* woman hovered in the shadows beside the divan. Padmini stood still, enduring their inspection. The servant glided forward. She was dressed in tight pantaloons, her heavy dark breasts bobbing free. Without a word she tore the bracelets from Padmini's trembling arms, then unwound the silk from the Indian girl's thin body. Dropping the items disdainfully on the floor, she moved back into the dark. The man ignored the proceedings completely, engrossed in his own thoughts, his eyes locked on infinity. The slave returned with some objects in her arms, and Padmini's breath caught at the sight of gold and jewels. Heavy gold bangles set with smooth jewels were slipped over her wrists. By the weight, and the greasy feel of some of the jewels she knew these were no fakes. The *kanak* slave knelt, and bangles were slipped onto one of her ankles. Larger and heavier, they clashed when she moved. Without looking, the *kanak* lashed her hand against Padmini's bare buttock. The Indian girl stood still. Rising, the slave pulled an open-fronted bodice onto Padmini's arms. It was of silk, heavily embroidered and worked with gold and set with pearls and diamonds. The gold scratched against her skin, and the diamonds, sewn throughout the lining as well as without, scraped harshly against her skin. Padmini looked down without moving and saw how the bodice framed and enhanced the color and soft texture of her breasts. Then an incredibly soft, diaphanous film of fabric was wrapped around her waist. Even in the dim light it did nothing to hide her person, merely emphasizing the darker shadow of her mound, the sleek curve of her thighs.

The *kanak* woman urged her forward, and Padmini, her heart quaking, stepped forward on the mat, her jewelry clinking. The man looked up at her, his face set in a harsh mask. Padmini approached the divan, her heart in her mouth, her breathing rapid, almost harsh. The other woman stopped her at the edge of the bed. While the man looked at Padmini fixedly, his eyes running leisurely and surely over her virginal form, the other woman knelt at his side. In her hand she held a narrow leather band. It caught the light and Padmini realized it was studded with smooth polished jewels. Using deft movements, the *kanak* woman wrapped the man's engorged phallus with the band. The head turned a darker red and swelled in the light, and the massive tower of flesh and stone rose threateningly from the darkness at the juncture of his thighs. Then Vivian was by her side. She forced the young Indian woman down on her back on the divan, beside the man. Then she slid down to Padmini's feet and held the girl's ankles apart in a firm grip. The man leisurely leaned over Padmini and mounted her. His toes dug into the bed, and his hands grasped Padmini's bangle-covered wrists, forcing them above her head, crushing them to the mattress. Now his body arced above hers, his eyes staring into her own. She peeked down between their bodies and saw his phallus aimed at the center of her being. Allowing her a brief moment to contemplate what was to come, he lowered his hips. The engorged head of his cock moved like a mechanical piston. For a second she felt the head nudge her outer lips pleasantly, but before she had had time to adjust, it was pushing into her, bruising the inner lips. When he met the thin membrane of her maidenhood she thought he would be stopped by this last barrier. Instead the head continued inexorably on, tearing her hymen with a pressing ripping feeling. The pain was exquisite. Sharp and delightful like nothing she had experienced before. He continued ramming forward, not allowing her the moment to herself. The cockhead pushed its way up her virginal channel, enlarging the space and tearing at her soft moist tissues. The studded leather followed, wringing still more sensation out of her bruised and torn membrane. She wailed, unable and unwilling to contain her feelings. The male face above her—her master, her lord—smiled into hers and she wailed her virginal song once again. She thought she could feel every stud, every vein, every touch of the head against her cunt and channel. When the cock was fully inserted in her, he suddenly precipitated his entire weight on her, jamming his cock even deeper into her young body. This time Padmini wailed her pain in earnest, and the scream and pain brought on clouds of greater pleasure. Finally, she and her prince were one. She wished to engulf him, to allow him to join with every inch of her, and without moving anything but the untutored muscles of her insides, she encouraged him to move into her. He did so savagely, taking his own pleasure from her pain and delight. She wailed encouragingly as his hips hammered into her, the ridges and bumps of the wrapping tearing again and again at her soft inexperienced flesh. Suddenly the combined pleasure and pain of his penetration was too much. With one final scream, Padmini fled into unconsciousness, knowing only that the pleasure of their bodies was continuing, and that his cock was hosing her insides with the white milk of his offering.

When she came to a few seconds later, she found him resting beside her. The phallus was still erect, and he was smiling at her, then bent to kiss her tear-bedecked cheeks, then, more deeply, her open mouth. The *kanak* slave came forward to release the bonds of his cock, but Padmini stopped her with an imperious hand. The phallus was hers now, hers to treat properly. She knelt between his legs, unrolling the sheathing carefully, worshipping it with reverence with her tongue as more and more of the thong-striped shaft was exposed. She could taste her virginal blood, the flavor of her insides, and of his bitter-salty juices on the shaft. Finally, in an act of complete obeisance, she filled her mouth and her throat with the entire length of the shaft, the hairs tickling her chin and nose, completely ignoring the gagging sensation at the back of her throat. She released the massive source of her pleasure only when it had softened and wilted. Even then, she released it reluctantly, her tiny tongue flicking her pleasure at every inch that slid out between her lips.

They lay together languorously while Vivian brought

tiny cups of fruit juices, slices of fish, and coconut delicacies.

"You were a maiden," he said, his chest rising in deep satisfaction.

"Yes," she sighed bashfully as was only appropriate. "I have been waiting for you, my prince."

"I know," he said, and she loved the sound of certainty and triumph in his voice, the voice of her conqueror.

They talked and snacked lightly. Their hands touched one another, stroking and enjoying the sensuous touch. Out of the corner of her eye Padmini saw that Orpheo's cock, which had wilted during the snack, was rising once again. He laughed to see her peek.

"Look at me fully," he commanded.

She obeyed instantly, her attention fully on the wondrous *lingam*. He lay on his side, the cock jutting horizontally out of his belly. With fearfully respectful fingers she caressed the maleness, barely conscious of Vivian exploring her own shaved *yoni*. Then she felt Vivian's tongue on the top of her slit, tickling the bruised little clitoral bud. The touch was soft, giving no hint of the fierceness that hid behind it. Padmini knew now what she herself was to do. Without hesitation, she bent forward and slipped the massive plum-head of Orpheo's cock into her mouth. Fully erect it was a monstrous presence in her oral cavity, and she could barely encompass it all. She felt his hand on her head and accepted that as an encouragement. With barely perceptible hollowing of her cheeks, she began sucking delicately at the tip. He pumped slightly into her, and she enlarged her mouth as much as she could, allowing the faint touch of her tiny perfect teeth to touch the skin. He shoved forward a bit more aggressively, and she loosened the muscles of her throat to allow the penetration. Then she held his belly in place with her hands and set herself to adoring the male member with her tongue. Her slim fingers found their way to her chin, and she cupped the soft hairy balls delicately, shuddering slightly at their furriness. But for the liquid sounds of the women's mouths, they enjoyed a moment of quiet. Then, when she was sure he was about to bless her with a load of his liquids, Orpheo pulled back from her. He rolled her over, raising her onto her knees and sending her face onto the cushions of the divan. Vivian climbed off the bed, returning immediately.

He parted the globes of her behind. Reaching in front of her, he showed Padmini what he held in his hand. It was a short, finger-thick horn of ivory. She looked at it for a moment. Its use was obvious, she thought, though why he would have to use something like that, she could not fathom: it was for old men who could no longer please their women, she knew from her reading. There was some movement behind her, then Vivian stepped out of the way. There was a look of anticipation on the *kanak* woman's face. It was only when the greased rod slid between her mounded buttocks that she realized where it was headed. He did not wait for her to adjust. The rod entered her rectum, parting the ring muscles easily. She groaned with the unfamiliarity of the penetration. Her prince started moving the artificial stem inside her. Not backwards and forwards, but twisting it about. The pain of the penetration grew, and this time she groaned with understanding and love.

Vivian, her face alight, knelt by the divan. She held

a large damascened box, its surfaces adorned with exquisite inlaid carvings of men and women engaged in sex. She opened it and showed Padmini the contents while the sudden touch of his lips, sucking at her buttocks, performed a counterpoint as the delicious ivory horn nailed her from behind.

There were more artificial cocks inside the box. They were of ivory, and stone, and gold. They nestled in velvet sockets, in two rows, and she saw that the smallest one was absent, ensconced, she knew, in her own asshole. The rods graduated from the size of a thick finger, to a circumference larger than her wrist. It was the second row that interested her more, however, that sent her pulse racing. The sockets in the second row were occupied by cocks that had been designed to stimulate to the full. The sizes differed. Here was one with a spiral of moonstones raising knobs on the shaft. A rod of silver was studded with thick black bristles, cut short, and she quailed at what that meant. The base of another consisted of tiny golden teeth. A fourth showed hairline sections, which, she knew, meant it was designed to be opened inside her. Inside *her*, she suddenly realized, and fear and expectation merged in her senses.

Orpheo examined the pert butt before him. Her buttocks, the color of butterscotch, were bisected by a line in the middle of which the ivory horn stuck up. Vivian was ramming the artificial cock back and forth into the butt hole. As she pulled it out, the strong anal muscles clung to the white shaft, reluctant to see it go. His cock rose, hardened even more than it had been. He seized a springy cane and brought it down across the tan expanse. A reddish welt rose and he raised the cane again, brought it whistling down to make a line perfectly parallel to the first one. The girl's shrieks melded with the splat of the cane into a melody of desire.

Padmini was not expecting the first stroke, and it caught her by surprise. Suddenly, there was a powerful blow on her rear, while it was still adjusting to the persistent violation by the ivory horn. The stroke seemed to reach somewhere from the base of her spine to the base of her skull.

"Guurk" was the only sound she could let out. The line of fire was eating into her skin, and she could already hear the sound of the second strike. She took refuge from the searing unexpected pain in the litany of her love.

"Oh! Oh, my lord! Oh lord!"

As the strokes started raining down on her upraised behind she began to feel the pleasure of this insistent beating.

"Oh yes, please lord. Oh my prince! Please lord. Aha, aha aha!"

Orpheo signaled to Vivian and she slipped beneath his arm to position herself on Padmini's other side. As she passed, she could not resist a loving bite at the sweat-slicked full lips that were framed by the buttocks: one marked with stripes, the other still virginal and unmarred. Then the cane, its rhythm unchanging, swished down again and ended with a splat on the taut skin. Orpheo continued his measured strokes until the second beautiful mound was as striped as the first. Vivian glanced at his cock. It was a fiery red, and so large it almost frightened her. Compassion for her co-lover overtook her, and she leaned back, covering the massive head with her lips, moistening it thoroughly with her spittle. She withdrew, and Orpheo, smiling slightly, struck her twice on her cheeks with the flat of his hand. She nodded, knowing he was not displeased with her action, but merely with her striving, if only in a small way, to usurp his role as master. He nodded to her again, and she pulled the ivory dildo out of the Indian woman's ass. The anal opening, widened by the horn, closed incompletely, and a dark narrow hole beckoned Orpheo. With a savage cry he struck one last time, then threw himself onto the trembling mounds. Unerringly his cock found its mark and drilled into the tight elastic hole. His hands went onto the mounds and pried them apart, making more room for his massive organ. In a second he had buried himself fully into her, his hair scraping against the lacerated buttocks. His teeth sought her shoulder and closed on the smooth honey flesh. Without waiting for her to adjust, he bucked in and out of her ass, his hips cushioned by the marvelously soft, trembling mounds of her rear. The tightness of her inner recesses was almost unbearable. His cock was in a vise. His balls slapped against her shaven mound, making a splatting sound that was barely heard above his harsh breathing and the woman's piteous cries. Then, as Vivian watched, cream gushed from his balls. Thick white syrup coated the shaft, squeezed out by the muscular action of his pumping rod and Padmini's tightened muscles. He rammed himself in once more, then rested for a second, before beginning his furious pumping once again.

The removal of the horn from her ass caused Padmini a brief moment of loss and panic. Then, suddenly, she found her ass being pulled apart by his strong hands. Without a word or motion of warning, she could feel the broad head of his cock at her rear entrance. She screamed a brief, unplanned scream of pain as the ravishing rod tore into her deepest recesses. He was like a bull in his demanding thrust, and his teeth closed on her neck like a male lion mounting his lioness. She responded with a deep-throated growl of delight. The pain in her backside was as nothing compared to the heights of pleasure she was now reaching. He pumped at her unremittingly, his hands parting her buttocks, tearing them with blunt nails. Then he gave one final thrust, and his sperm gushed into her rectum. She was nowhere near her own climax, but she relaxed as much as possible, only slightly disappointed. The flush of cream in her ass smoothed the agony somewhat, but the bites on her shoulder did not cease, and then she realized that he had no intention of dismounting. His cock was as hard as before, except that now the shaft was lubricated by his cream, and the pleasure flared in her, spurred by the burning sensation on her buttocks, and the great stretching, tearing hole between them. His lips left her shoulder, and his powerful hands grasped them instead, then released her. He rocked back onto her supine frame.

Orpheo's entire weight pinned her by the shaft in her ass to the divan. He rocked above her, supported by the concubine, while he drilled her full of his maleness. Padmini screamed with pleasure at the use of her body. She clawed at the divan, tearing her nails into the tough fabric as her own climax hit and her insides churned like the insides of a volcano. Her climax ended with a series of deep shudders that caused him to grab her shoulder heavily to avoid being thrown.

Without waiting for her to completely recover her composure, Padmini felt him withdraw from her inner recesses. He seated himself on one of the hard bolsters on the bed, His cock stuck out before him, hard, thick and shiny, the prominent veins glistening in the light. Padmini immediately knew what to do.

She seated herself on him, holding her body up by effort that stood the ligaments of her thighs out into bronze cables under her skin. The massive cock disappeared up her rectum, and she could feel every agonizing, pleasure-giving inch as it worked its way up her insides. His hands went around her back, and he eased his passage by pulling her buttocks apart. Then he slid his hands higher up her torso.

"Lash her," Padmini's prince said, his voice muffled between her breasts. Padmini looked behind her. The *kanak* slave stood impassively behind their backs, and Padmini craned her neck at a faint chinking sound. Light glinted on the silver coils in the slave's hands. Lengths of fine silver chain hung from the large fist. The slave, unconscious of Padmini's regard, was dreamily running the links over her own large breasts. She caught a nipple between the links and squeezed hard. The other strands jingled a muffled sound and the black nipple grew darker, accentuated against the silver of the chains. The slave raised her hand, her eyes blank, her parted lips moist. Padmini tensed involuntarily, and Orpheo pulled her to him, their flesh meshing moistly. "It is silver," he said. "Soft, malleable, light."

She felt rather than heard the swish of the chain strands through the air. The chains bit into her skin with a pain that was almost, but not quite, unbearable. She sucked in her breath as tears came to her eyes. The hot hard phallus was still probing her tender behind, thrust into her inner recesses like a glowing bar. The chains swished through the air again and splatted against her mounded buttocks. She cried out at the double agony, but held her place with sheer effort of will. Then the lashing speeded up, burning into her flesh and she was lost in a blaze of lustful pain. His hands grasped her tits, thumbing the nipples back into the mounds of flesh, then pulling her down onto him. Again she cried out at the penetration deeper into her anal channel. And the lashes continued to rain down on her buttocks, biting deeply.

From deep within her Padmini could feel the rise of a monster of heat and pleasure. It rose from the screwing motion of the penis in her behind, from the intense stripes of disjointed pain that rocked her ass, from the grasping feel of his hands rough on her breasts. When he pulled himself up, using nothing but his belly muscles and kissed her nipples softly and lovingly, she was ready. Her thighs went around his hips, her head went back and a long cry of pain and ecstasy broke out. The shaft in her behind throbbed and pulsed, and soothing fluid gushed into her ass while his mouth engulfed and encompassed first one reddened breast and then the other. With a volcanic orgasm that almost jolted her from the peg of his cock, she felt her insides cream and quivers of violent pleasure ran through her body. In her victory she clawed her nails onto his exposed skin, drawing bright red marks, the brand of her ownership.

It was close to dawn and the night was turning light. She climbed the stairs with trembling limbs. Dropping the sari she almost fell into bed, then remembered that her mother checked on her room first thing every morning. She staggered to the closet and folded the soft cloth, then fell into bed, unaware that her bedroom door was slightly open.

Chapter 8

The day had been exceptionally humid, and her raw insides had responded pleasantly to the torture of waiting for evening. Padmini had loitered as long as she could in her bath, then she had put on her worn robe and drifted silently in bare feet, over the polished wood of the corridor to her room. Beneath she could hear the high-pitched voice of her mother and the lower bass of her father as they talked in Hindi. They were probably talking about their perennial problem: herself. And her lack of a suitable husband.

In her own narrow room she dropped the robe and posed naked before the mirror. The sun was about to set and it cast dappled shadows through the palm trees onto her bed. There were drops of moisture on her skin, but outwardly she looked no different. It was only inside that she knew she was now no longer as her parents saw her. No longer a shy virgin, but the consort of the prince she had waited for all her life. She parted her lower lips. The hole stung when she inserted her finger, but the annoying bit of skin was no longer there. With another finger she explored the other, rear entrance, pushing her slender brown finger in to the knuckle, reveling in the touch and the slight pain in both her entrances. Her eyes closed as she rubbed herself, touching the tips of her breasts with her other hand.

Padmini heard a sound behind her, which drew her back from her reverie. She turned to see Radh, his eyes wide in shock. Her hand flashed to the towel, then stopped. The look in his eyes was a strange mixture. She could see his shock at the sight of her bruised buttocks. But beneath the shock she could see something else, the glint of approval and of…of…lust. Her eyes were drawn to the bulge in his *dhoti*. His lips parted and she could see the sudden rise and fall of his slender muscular chest. She turned her body to face him, feeling the bounce of her breasts, noticing, through half-closed lids that his interest quickened. The marks of the chains on her breasts had not faded yet, she knew. He drew a sharp breath as she swayed toward him, shock clear on his face. Padmini reached behind her brother, making sure she brushed his body with her breast as she did so, and closed the door. Then she stepped away from him, supporting her breasts with her hands, thumbs caressing the nipples. Her feet slightly parted, eyes lowered, she waited for his next move.

His face darkened with blood. "You have been…" he said, unable to continue. "You…my sister! Who with?" He hissed the words through clenched teeth, and she had time to notice how beautifully white they were in his dark face. "Who was it? Hey? Who...?" A froth of spittle gathered at the corners of his mouth. Padmini smiled, and merely stroked her breasts with both hands. Her nipples felt as if they were bursting out of her skin.

Suddenly he lashed her across the face with the flat of his hand. Perhaps he had expected her to cry out, to beg. He did not expect her to take a deep breath, smile fully in his face and raise her own to his, a half smile on her parted lips.

"Again!" she said, half demanding.

He slapped her again, halfheartedly. The pain was exquisite, a start on the pleasure she expected. She retreated from him, and as expected, Radh interpreted her retreat as fear of his attack and he advanced. She knelt on her narrow bed, presenting her full-moon ass to him. Her damp hair was undone and it hung partly over her face as she turned and implored him over her shoulder: "More!"

Enraged, Radh advanced and rained slaps on her upraised buttocks, his eyes trying, but not succeeding, in evading the sight of her pudgy nether lips, still inflamed by the shafting she had received.

"Whore," he muttered. "You dishonor..." he was starting to shout when he realized that their parents downstairs might hear him. "Show some respect," he whispered between clenched teeth, seizing her shoulder and spinning her around on the bed.

Padmini fell back and parted her legs, her eyes shining. Radh, breathing heavily through his nose looked fully for the first time at his sister. She was leaning back on one elbow, making an enticing picture. Her breasts were mounded against her thin rib cage, a paler brown than her arms and face. Her hips swelled, and her parted thighs, slightly raised, led his gaze to the source of pleasure. Her shaven mound was dark and the slit between the full lips darker still, but inside the dark slit could be seen a dark red, just peeking out, glistening in the light of the covered lamp. Padmini's eyes were staring, glowing in the reflected light.

When her slim hand stole down her belly, heading for the crack, Radh broke from his paralysis. He took one long step forward to the bed and his hand fell fully onto her mound in a resounding slap.

She giggled softly, squirming with the blow. "Ah, Oh...again. Oh. Quietly, they'll hear..."

He rained blows on her sex and she squirmed with the power of them. Tears burst from his eyes in frustration, and he became suddenly conscious of the massive erection inside his *dhoti*. As if she could read his mind, Padmini's gaze fixed on his bulging crotch. Barely knowing what he was doing, Radh tore at the tie of cloth and the baggy cover fell to the floor. With a hoarse cry he fell forward between her welcoming thighs. She buried her mouth in his muscular shoulder and shrieked into his brown sweaty skin as she felt the magnificent manstalk penetrate the squishy moisture of her insides.

Radh felt himself falling into his sister's arms. His raging cock searched out the softness between her legs. The sensation was unlike anything he had ever felt before with a woman. Padmini's hands clawed at his back in a frenzy, while her tight tube fought his penetration. Her inner tissues parted reluctantly from his assault and he heard her screams through a red haze that covered his vision. His pubic bone ground against hers, and his wiry nether hair ground into her shaven cunt eliciting another cry and bite from her. He pulled back and his mouth fastened on hers, striking into her oral cavern with his tongue and lips. She cried out again, safe in the knowledge that his mouth muffled the sounds. Rocking fiercely, he pulled out slightly and rammed again into her bruised cunt. His hands grasped her buttery ass, squeezing with all their might, bruising the soft flesh. She bit his lips and he pulled back with a cry of pain and bent his neck to her full tit, biting down on the prominent nipple. Slamming into her powerfully again and again, he could feel her entire inner channel quiver at his assault. He fell forward on her, pressing her down into the mattress with his entire weight, then pulling his cock out, horrified at what he had done.

As if misunderstanding his motives entirely, Padmini immediately rolled over onto her hands and knees, burying her face in the pillow. Radh's rage flared up anew. His hands rained blows on Padmini's upraised moons, striking and pinching her skin in a delightful glissade of blows that sent roaring pleasure to her hindbrain. She arched her back, presenting more of her dark crannies to the blows. With a cry of outraged frustration, he fell forward onto her back. His erect prick, darker than the rest of his skin, pierced her waiting cunt. It ripped into her orifice and he slammed forward with all the power and anger he possessed. Their entangled bodies crashed forward, her thin arms unable to support the brutality of the assault. Flat on the bed, Radh felt his cock pulsing uncontrollably. A wave of undeniable pleasure gushed from his full balls. With a low cry he pulled back and tried to control the hosing of his sister's insides.

Padmini felt the man over her stiffen, and she knew that his crisis was near, far ahead of herself. Then suddenly he was pulling back, and she felt masses of hot sperm spurting over her buttocks and back, almost sizzling on her heated skin. She bit into the pillow, hoping for more, her own climax almost but not quite arriving as well. Instead she felt the inert weight of her brother fall again over her and his hot breath on her shoulder.

The weight was becoming uncomfortable when Radh pulled back and staggered to his feet. They looked at one another for a moment, she peering happily over her bite-marked shoulder, he clutching his betraying organ, and then he turned and left without a word. Humming to herself, Padmini took her towel and softly wiped the residue of their love-making from between her thighs and from her back. She dipped one finger into a small pool of come and flicked it with the tip of her tongue. She made a face. A taste she would have to get used to.

After dark, making some excuse to her family she went to the house on the point. He was there, waiting. He smiled as she called her greeting and walked into the house. Her voice was barely louder than the susurrus of the palm trees above the roof. Orpheo beckoned her closer, examining her as she approached patiently and waited for his orders.

"You are unhappy and disturbed," he said finally, his fingers feather touching her shoulders, her cheeks, the lengths of her arms.

Padmini nodded wordlessly. She could smell the male sweat of his body.

Orpheo raised his head and stared blindly off into the dark beams of the ceiling, as if his gaze could pierce the roof of the hut. He ran a thumb around her dark jaw. She shivered involuntarily.

At a silent gesture, Vivian approached out of the dark. She was naked, and the signs of their lovemaking lay on her clearly. Her shoulders were marked by deep bites and there were faint weals on the front of her thighs. Padmini's heart lurched with jealousy, and as if divining her thoughts, his stroking hands slapped her breasts rapidly, with the speed of a striking snake. Her attention focused on him again, and even when Vivian's body, smelling of intermingled female and male sweat and the bitter flavor of his sperm was pressed against her, still she kept her attention on her prince.

Orpheo said something in *kanak*, then turned Padmini's frame. They watched, she conscious of his breathing onto her nape, as Vivian rubbed herself all over with oil. The deep heavy smell of coconut oil, mixed with some flowery fragrance permeated the hut. Vivian swayed over to the chest by the divan and fumbled there in the dimness. Orpheo's hands were on Padmini's slim rib cage. Her heart was beating wildly under his strong palms, and she could feel the weight of her unbound breasts against the back of his hands. Behind her, his cock, in full erection as always, pressed into the fissure of her behind. She nestled into his arms, awaiting events.

Padmini drew a deep breath when Vivian turned to face them. Under her large soft breasts rose an enormous golden cock. It gleamed and glinted as she stepped into the pool of light cast by a lamp hanging from the beams overhead. It was studded with jewels that winked at Padmini's fascinated eyes, and she knew that the original for the gold-veined model strapped to the woman's belly was even now throbbing behind her.

Orpheo stepped slightly back. His hands rose, then suddenly descended. Her dress ripped, the cotton pulling against her shoulders. She wore no underwear under the print. Vivian strode to her and grasped the shreds still hanging from her shoulders. Pulling forward and down, the rags pooled at her feet. She had a moments regret at the dress, but that emotion vanished with the threatening approach of the giant phallus.

Padmini knew what she had to do. She knew she had to abase herself before the slave. Because it was her master's wish. Her arms rose and her hands clasped the back of her neck in contempt, showing off her perfect form for the slave.

"Here I am," she cried. "Look at me. Do what you want." She cast a look of contempt at the slave.

Vivian looked at Padmini for a moment, a faint smile on her lips, considering the rags of her dress which contrasted so with the contemptuous tones. Then her firm large hands grasped Padmini's prominent nipples and twisted them viciously. Padmini shrieked a muffled cry that came from behind her clamped jaws. From behind, her prince clasped her belly, his fingers sliding toward her little pearl nubbin. Vivian's head lowered toward the nipples and her teeth ground against the sensitive flesh, while her powerful lips sucked at the prominent black nubbin and her fingers crushed the sensitive flesh of one nipple between thumb and finger. Padmini's pleasure was increased when she felt her prince's hands squeezing her buttocks. He was merciless in his explorations, seeking out the remains of the weals from her previous beating and pinching them.

Vivian cried something out in *kanak*. She seized the Indian woman by her hips and dragged her to the wide couch. The two women fell onto the embroidered silk cover. Vivian's full weight came down on the slimmer girl's frame. She reached between their bodies to find the tip of the artificial phallus. Then her fist sought Padmini's moist entrance.

The knob the slave was intending to use on her seemed tremendous, but Padmini knew it was an exact copy of her prince's *lingam*. Nonetheless she felt a frisson of fear. She knew the slave would use the opportunity to get back at her. The slave lunged forward. The massive unyielding artificial cock plunged into Padmini's recently-widened hole. The full weight of the slave's body slammed down onto Padmini's delicate frame. Then the slave's head was pulled aside and her prince's face loomed in its stead. He pulled Padmini's face to him, his lips seeking hers just as his own warm sword plunged into Vivian's cunt. Together they set out to fuck the dark girl that lay beneath them, their combined strengths making her body tremble on the bed with each thrust. Padmini thought she would suffocate, but along with the feeling of suffocation came a pleasure so intense, she did not know if the difficulty she had breathing was the result of the force or her own pleasure. Wild grunts and shrieks emerged from her throat and were immediately swallowed by the demanding mouth that covered her own.

Vivian was shoved roughly aside as Orpheo approached his climax. Usually he took his time, but there was a peculiar urgency to his moves now. His hips thrust forward then twisted into Padmini's widened channel. She squirmed lasciviously beneath him, her mouth stuck to his own. Vivian joined in, her teeth and hands aiding the lovers until Orpheo suddenly stiffened. Vivian slid a hand between his thighs to touch his hairy balls and was rewarded with the feeling of his sac contracting rhythmically and showering Padmini's insides with his thick creamy spermal fluid. He withdrew slowly, and Vivian, her fingers barely circling the shaft, squeezed the gluey fluid onto the Indian girl's waiting cunt, then anointed the shaft of the cock she still wore. Orpheo stepped out from between Padmini's parted legs. He looked at the gaping, oozing pink entrance, framed by sweat slicked thighs. Padmini's eyes looked at him, unfathomable pools of femininity.

"Mount her again," he commanded Vivian. "Fuck her! Fuck her hard!" he said, then left the room. Gladly, Vivian mounted the complaisant body of the waiting girl. The cream-anointed knob slid easily into the expectant soft hole, and her heavy breasts mashed down on Padmini's smaller ones.

Radh had followed Padmini through the dark. He had lost her in the labyrinth of small gardens and houses that was a *kanak* neighborhood at the edge of the town. Then some instinct had driven him to the unpopulated area around Taulea Point. He knew the *kanak* as well as the Indian population avoided the area after dark. It had been the site of one of the *kanak* temples, and spirits were still supposed to live there. And old Ta was reputed to have dangerous magic at his command; even the Indian community feared him.

There was a single large house hidden by a masking

reed wall. It was larger than most *kanak* houses, and enclosed as well. As he passed he thought he heard a familiar voice. He stopped, then sneaked into the garden and up onto the porch. The voice came again, this time crying out in the sound of pleasure he had heard before. So! Finally he had found her. The blood boiled in his veins, as his own lust and rage turned to jealousy. For a moment he forgot what had happened before, in their parents' house, and was only the brother out to guard his sister's honor. He raised his hand to hammer furiously at the wooden door that barred his entrance. The door was not there. Instead a deeper darkness loomed, and beyond the figure of a man Radh could hear the passionate cries that sounded like his sister.

"Yes?" a deep voice spoke in Hindi. "You are Radh," the voice said with finality, then added in English. "You are punctual. That is excellent." The figure was moving away from him, toward a dimly outlined doorway, and Radh hurriedly followed, his anger and fear driving him inexorably.

They turned into a large, dimly lit room. A brighter light shone like a spot on a wide divan scattered with embroidered silken cushions. Rugs and silk hangings adorned the wall. Carved chests were scattered on the floor, some of them bearing antique Indian pieces of brass, washed gold, and ivory. Radh's training in his father's shop automatically made a rapid tally. The worth of this room was probably higher than their entire stock. Radh knew that his cogitations were a simple attempt to deny the rest of what his eyes were seeing. The spot shone on two entwined, naked female figures. And one of them was Padmini.

"Come here!" the man commanded Radh.

Step by step, as if forced at gunpoint, Radh approached the bed. Padmini was lying on the divan, her legs spread. A *kanak* girl was lying on top of her, her mouth busily and hungrily moving at his sister's lips. The *kanak* woman's large hands were gripping Padmini's breasts, twisting the delicate buds about. Padmini's eyes, those deep black pools, were closed by her incredibly long lashes. And the *kanak* girl was pumping at his sister's hips, her ass moving in long curves, as if she was a man.

"Look!" the man commanded, and went to stand at the foot of the divan, peering without expression between the women's legs. "Isn't she beautiful?"

Trembling violently, Radh considered fleeing, then, instead, found his feet directing him to stand beside the man.

"Look at her *yoni*. The perfect shape. And her breasts were made for the male mouth. Consider how those small bruises enhance the smooth beauty of her skin," he added in Hindi again.

Radh's trembling grew, and he could not take his eyes away from the splayed figure on the divan.

"It is actually your sister that you want, isn't it?" The cool voice was absolutely certain. Radh shivered, wanting to protest, then suddenly realized there was no one to protest to. The girl lay before him, her legs spread wide. Darkly she invited him, with the only paleness the half-moons glinting beneath her lids.

"Closer!" the man commanded.

Radh moved forward until the smell of the women's sweat rose in his nostrils. He could see tiny beads of sweat on Padmini's upper lip, and hear her tiny satisfied grunts as the *kanak* woman's butt muscles shafted the artificial cock into her.

Tau'tevu

A hand on his shoulder forced him to bend and examine the action at a close remove. He had never seen a woman's cunt in action before. The dark shaft, gnarled with vein-like projections, was slick and shiny with his sister's secretions. As it rammed forward the inner lips bulged and the cunt-hole opened. Then as the woman reversed direction, he saw the same inner lips grip hungrily at the shaft, reluctant to let the morsel go. Fascinated, his hands stole on their own volition to the exquisite skin, and he pressed the fat outer lips onto the shaft. He heard Padmini groan as his fingers stroked her most secret parts. His other hand grasped the muscular rump of the woman who was fucking Padmini. It was firm and soft in turn as the woman flexed and released her muscles, driving into the one beneath her. Another, slimmer hand grasped his exploring one. Padmini drove her blunt nails deeply into the back of his hand, forcing his own fingers into the unknown woman's ass muscles. The *kānak* shrieked, and her thrusts became deeper and more powerful. Padmini cried out, and scratched at his hand again.

"More! More!" Padmini was crying and her hand directed Radh's hand into the sensitive recesses of the *kanak* woman's ass.

Fascinated, Radh experimented with his control over the speed and force of the two women's movements. His own pulse was hammering in his head, and he was conscious that his cock was erect and pushing against the material of his cotton pants. He was suddenly angry, angry at both the women, lusting after both of him. His hand rose and descended in a powerful slap. The dark woman turned her head and her eyes blazed at him. He slapped her again, then again, and her head rose. From her open mouth came a howl of pleasure and joy and the speed of her fucking increased. Beneath her Radh could see Padmini moving, gasping, howling herself with the power of the *kanak*'s thrusts. His blows fell on the fat quivering backside muscles like the rattle of a machine gun. Briefly, then, he saw the man blocking his vision, pulling the *kanak* woman off Padmini. The small dark Indian girl was spread before him. Her belly was quivering and she was calling out hoarsely. Her shaved mound was slick with juices, and her cunt hole was still open and ready to accommodate the shaft. He hit out, wildly, perversely, at the quivering belly and the slick lips alike.

"Oooaaah!" Padmini made no effort to protect herself. Her heels dug into the coverlet and she arched her belly and cunt up to him, meeting and demanding his blows. A hand was on Radh's pants, pulling them expertly to his knees.

"Mount her!" an undeniable voice commanded.

He tried to object, tried to remember that there was some reason for him not to have this woman before him, then he was on his knees between the spread legs, his hand on his cock. He positioned his slim cock before the entrance, the delicious smells of woman-sex rising in his nostrils. For a moment he tried to stop himself, then suddenly a flaming stripe crossed his buttocks. He screamed his rage and fell forward.

Radh thrust himself into the waiting body beneath him. Padmini wailed softly, not in complaint, and he thrust again in a frenzy, his cock filling the lubricious channel. Over his shoulder, Vivian stood with a lash in her hands. Her body was tense with denied lust. Orpheo had pulled her away just as she was reaching her orgasm, and the frustration of the moment was translating itself to rage. She lashed, blindly at first, then when she saw that she could control his movements as he had controlled hers, she calmed down and struck with more precision. Each blow landed across the tight skin raising a welt just as the man thrust downwards. Padmini's pink mouth was open, her white teeth shone in her face that expressed gratification and gratitude at Vivian's actions. She started coming, her belly quivering in spasms that translated directly into the clutching grip of her knees and thighs around the man.

Radh felt Padmini's orgasm. Her hands pulled at his shoulders, and the burning slashes against his buttocks drove him into a frenzy. He cried out, finding that his own sperm was rising from his balls into an undeniable and incredible sensation along the length of his shaft. Radh looked down and saw a copy of his own face twisted into a lascivious grimace of overwhelming pleasure, and his cock shot off into the clenching depths of the warm cunt. He slapped Padmini's face, tears of anger mixed with shame and lust coursing down his cheeks. "Whore!" he shouted. "Slut!" and slapped her face again from side to side several times. Tears came to her face, she gulped but the grinding movement of her pelvis against his never stopped. He grabbed her breasts violently, the full soft brown flesh bulging between his fingers, and she screamed quietly, then her nails dug into his buttocks, drawing blood and he resumed his attack, spitting all the words he knew into her wide-eyed face, mauling her breasts with his hands.

Radh woke to find himself alone in the hut, in a plainly furnished room. He staggered from the bed to find a breakfast tray—sweetmeats, *lassi,* coffee, and fruit—waiting on a low table. Refreshed, still not believing the events of the previous night, he walked through the growing light of dawn back to his parents' house. He walked in before anyone in the household had begun the day. He was the last unmarried son, and no one questioned his coming and going. He stopped at Padmini's door. It was slightly open. Within, she lay in her bed, her face pillowed on one arm, a soft smile on her face. He turned to go and missed the quick mischievous wink from her half-closed lids.

Chapter 9

Drawn again, despite himself, to the dark native hut on Taulea Point, Radh stared blearily through the dark. He had been drinking, something he had never done before. Throughout the day he had moved in somewhat of a daze, avoiding acquaintances and friends, not really seeing the white and pink flesh of the tourists on the beach where he wandered. He had brandies at one bar, and when that had palled, had moved down the beach for another drink, then even to a *kanak* drinking place, where, notwithstanding semi-hostile stares, he had consumed several cups of *kava*, which had numbed his lips but neither his mind nor his cock. Now he was standing at the darkened entrance to the porch. A dim glow was cast by an intricate cage of woven grasses which held a swarm of fireflies. Angrily he batted at the caged insects, then felt ashamed at letting his anger and frustration out on the friendly little insects. He heard, faintly, the sound of a *vina* being played, and also, and his heart pounded at the knowledge, the high-voiced giggle of female voices, one of whom he was sure was his sister, and the deep rumble of a male voice.

His anger and impetuosity rose as he strained his ears. His drunkenness had almost evaporated, leaving him with little more than hot eyes and anger. He pushed his way roughly to the entrance. It opened before him, not even locked. The house seemed dark, yet there was a flickering glint of light from one of the inner rooms. He marched through some hangings, intending to have it out with his sister and her lover.

He stormed into the room, then stopped. The sounds he had been hearing, which he had known to be his sister turned out to be an Indian soap opera. The television flicker was the only light in the room. On the divan, which he had consciously avoided looking at, the sight of his shame, lay a figure. He strode over, and the *kanak* girl, the one who had been with them on the previous occasion, stirred in her sleep. She was naked but for a shell necklace and armbands, and a wreath around her hair.

He stared at the helpless figure for a second, embarrassed to see her so. She stirred. One of her knees rose in her sleep as she adjusted to a new posture. In the flickering light he could see her curly bush, and the dark lips of her cunt. Her hand lay flat on her belly, with the large fingers on the top of her mound. His erection, which had softened at the sight of the TV rose again, and he remembered her mocking grin and the delight she had taken when he had abused Padmini. His heart was pounding in his chest, and suddenly the spirit of madness took over again. He threw off his *dhoti*, and without removing his shorts, pulled her knees apart and immediately lunged forward.

Her channel was moist and tight. Different, he realized, from Padmini's though he could not fully identify the difference. Then it came to him: her wiry, bushy hairs were scraping against his shaft as he thrust home. He drove fully up her before she managed to wake and respond.

"You bastard," she panted under him, trying to reach his eyes with her fingers. He fought her off, his cock pounding roughly into her. He grabbed both her wrists with his hands and pinned her to the bed with his hips and the weight of his body. She struggled under him and he bit her full breast to teach her a lesson. The bite only intensified her struggles, and his cock was almost jerked from within her slicked channel. She cried out and tried to avoid his lips when his mouth sought hers and Radh roughly twisted her hands behind her back until he could grab both with one hand.

With his free hand Radh grabbed the mass of frizzy hair and pulled her head far back. Then he began slapping her breasts while his hips kept on pounding into the moistened tight entrance, which, in its attempts to resist him, clamped onto his cock like a vise.

"You bitch!" he called in a harsh whisper. "You debauched my sister! Bitch, bitch!" with each word he slapped her harder. The dark nipples in their large aureoles sprang erect and a reddish blush covered the full mounds. Wordlessly she snarled at him.

Radh was almost crying now. "Whore!" he cried.

"Fuck you, you whore! You are no better than a dog!" The rain of blows came down on her skin like hailstones on a tin roof.

The sudden weight had only been partly expected. Nonetheless, Vivian had enjoyed the vicious thrust which had heralded Radh's assault. Lying there, with Padmini in her arms, waiting for Radh to arrive at his unanticipated assignation, Padmini had giggled, "He has a lot of suppressed violence in him. Poor man, not knowing whether he is Indian or Tau'tevan. He will fuck and beat you very well."

Vivian had smiled hopefully in the dimness.

Now that Radh was a hot demanding reality on her body, she threw herself fully into the role. She knew it was her duty to repel this foreign chieftain, and like a good *vahine* she fought with all her strength. The cock slamming into her gave her only a part of the pleasure she needed, and when he twisted her hands behind her, she did not resist as hard as she could. The first slap on her breast had been a pleasant and stimulating shock. This new chief was serious about his assault, and she set out to make it as hard as possible for him. Her hands rose and scraped at the skin of his shoulders in a frenzy, bringing blood. He slapped her again and again while his rigid tool shafted deeply into her and she felt the inner lips of her cunt extend and grip the intruder.

Radh was angry now, and the anger was transforming itself into a driving movement that caused the woman under him to shudder and tremble with each thrust. His teeth were fastened on one of the full breasts now, and he bit with abandon, raising red welts.

The woman was crying and pushing at his head, causing his neck tendons to stand out.

There was movement beside him. He looked around from the corner of his eye. The man who was his sister's lover was kneeling on the bed, an impassive look on his hawk-face. He was completely naked, and seeing Radh's attention on him, he lay back on the bed, his head propped by a pillow.

"Mount me," the other man commanded, and suddenly Radh's sister was there. She too was naked, but for bangles that adorned her wrists and ankles, and which chimed as she moved. Her dark eyes, which she kept on Radh, were fathomless. She squatted in her full nudity next to the man, displaying her dark, hairless cunt, then opening it to his view with her fingers. The pink cleft and sweet hole were fully exposed, glowing softly amidst the almost black of her lips. Then she straddled the waiting prick of the supine man. Holding the knob with her fingers, she rubbed it first between the lips and Radh unwillingly witnessed them parting in desire as the red knob pressed between them. Padmini reached behind her, and inserted the knob firmly inside herself, then slid down the pale pole until the hairs tickled her denuded and distended cunt labia. Orpheo did not move, and knowing her duty, she began rising and falling on the erect shaft. The brown shaft emerged, glinting with her internal juices, and her face was twisted in pleasure. She bent forward, rubbing her breasts lasciviously against Orpheo's chest, her hands digging first into her own lush backside, then into the hard muscles of his chest.

Radh's attention was now split, unevenly, between

the *kanak* who had him in the grip of her thighs, and the giggling figure of Padmini next to him. She rode the man's supine figure, raising herself to expose the length of cock, then dropping down in a perfect rhythm. Her eyes were partly on her partner, partly on him, and his cock jerked in response. The speed of his movements increased and now he was not aiming at hurting the woman beneath him, but in finding his own pleasure. The *kanak* girl beneath him was breathing heavily, exhaling with a sigh each time his weight came down upon her. He explored her lush figure with his fingers, and then with his lips. Finally his lips descended on her mouth for a deep and soul-satisfying kiss. This was the first time, he found, that he had actually kissed a native of the island. His demanding hands grew bolder, and she aided his movements, raising her hips when he gripped her behind, clenching her hands on his so that his strong thin fingers buried themselves deeply into her willing soft flesh, the tips of his middle fingers driving into the dryer, muscular zone of her anal button.

Before he was completely ready, Radh found himself approaching a climax. Beneath him, the woman too was beginning to pant, and her eyes rolled up in her head. He clasped her strongly to his demanding hips, and his mouth clamped onto hers, exploring the warm cavern of her mouth with his tongue and teeth.

Radh felt his balls empty themselves of everything, bury themselves as deeply as possible into the waiting hungry cunt. The *kanak* girl was screaming something into his shoulder, a shoulder that was marked all over with the horseshoe mark of her bites. Beside them he was vaguely conscious that the man under his sister was emptying himself into her, arching his hips deeply into her expectant loins. When he had finally collapsed onto the willing body of his *vahine* he turned to face the other couple. Padmini was lying in abandon on her lover. His cock was lying glistening on his thigh. Blobs of white semen hung in driblets about the Indian girl's dark entrance, and more was oozing sluggishly out.

At the sight of the violation Radh's rage and anger returned, he rolled off the woman and reached for Padmini. There was a tangle of limbs and he found himself facing Padmini's full-moon ass, the dribs of come clotting on the expensive coverlet. Orpheo was standing near them. In his hands he held long strands of raffia woven together at one end to form a handle. He held the instrument out to Radh, who took it uncertainly, then looked at his sister's wanton exposure, at the gamin smile she flashed at him, mockingly, over her shoulder. The *kanak* crawled over the bed, pulling Padmini's head to her, burying it between the thighs that still reeked of Radh's own semen and lustful sweat. Her eyes fully upon him, while her large fist held Padmini's head down by the hair, she licked her lips.

"Beat her!" Orpheo commanded. "You are her brother, her lover. She has been with another. Beat her!"

Padmini was spread between them. Her head was hidden between Vivian's thighs. Her ankles in their heavy gold anklets, were held apart firmly by Orpheo. The traces of the man's cream were visible, white and glistening on the dark, almost black lips between his sister's dark thighs.

Still he hesitated.

"Another man!" Orpheo insisted. "Not you, another! Punish her!"

Padmini twisted wildly between the imprisoning thighs, muttering indistinct words. It was the squirming movement of her behind, the behind he had wanted to love and touch, the behind she had touched so brutally before the mirror, that finally galvanized him to action. His hand rose, the unfamiliar weight of the *muloko'ewa* flapping back, then brought it down in a tentative strike at the brown mounds.

Padmini squirmed in anticipation. Vivian's imprisoning thighs formed a private, dark, comforting world for her vision, she could smell her brother's discharges on the thighs, and tentatively licked at the dripping come. And she eagerly waited the touch of whatever would follow. The first stroke was a pale ghost of what she expected. She squirmed in anger, ashamed at the light touch, yelled imprecations in Hindi, and when those were muffled by Vivian's thick thighs, she bit the tender brown skin with all her might. Her reward was immediate and gratifying, and she leaped at the full blow of a hand on her lower back. Her noises must have aroused Radh, for the strength of his blows immediately increased.

Radh saw the *kanak* woman jump suddenly and cry out. Her hand rose and slapped hard, down on what she could reach of Padmini's buttocks, then again. The slaps were like pistol shots, and Padmini writhed in response. Radh, conscious of *why* he was there, raised the lash suddenly, his pulse pounding at the sounds of the women, and brought the *muloko'ewa* down as hard as he could on the soft pale brown buttocks, leaving a series of thin parallel welts. Then again, until he was beating her in a frenzy of excitation. His cock was again at full erection, painful in its intensity. His blows increased and the weight of his swaying penis added to the intensity of the feel as the lash cut into the soft flesh of Padmini's ass.

"I'm going to lash you into rags," he hissed. "It will be terrible, a fit punishment for your sin," and he raised the lash once again only to bring it down on her soft flesh.

"Oh, that beautiful sound. Yes, again, again, I must!" his voice was hoarse and he could barely control himself from throwing his full weight onto her quivering body.

Tears were running down her full cheeks, but Radh did not have the time to examine them. Vivian grabbed his erect member suddenly, and drew him inexorably to the waiting opening. He sank down into Padmini's depths. She was tight, but so wet he felt like he was sinking into a fathomless sea. His whole frame trembled. He cried out hoarsely, and his cock immediately started pumping his fluid into the already fully inundated channel that enclosed him. His eyes and teeth were clenched, and his hands grasped repeatedly into the soft buns before him, feeling the raised welts, while his ears heard Padmini's moans and cries of pain and pleasure.

When it was over, he hurriedly rolled off the exhausted slight body, still shocked at what he had done. The island woman nestled close beside him, and placed one of his hands on her breast, the other on Padmini's quivering ass. She smiled.

"Vivian," she said.

"Huh?" He looked at her.

"Vivian. My name is Vivian. Since you've raped me, it's only right that you be able to address me as well."

Radh laughed, a swelling belly laugh that convulsed him on the bed. The tension broke and the others laughed with him. Padmini, her cheeks still streaked with tears, doubled over and kissed the tip of his prick, and he idly stroked her fine long hair in appreciation.

Chapter 10

Sara was beginning to feel that the vacation on Tau'tevu was turning into a bust. The first three nights had been fine. She had had some idea of picking up one of the natives, and they had eyed her in return. But Jo and she had met some fellows from Sydney, and the four of them had been together since. The boys had been staying at a cheap hostel, so Sara and Jo's room had soon become their hangout. At night the two couples had humped in the dark room, Sara, conscious of the moans and stirrings from the next bed, as she was conscious of her own sounds as Stan fucked her. And conscious too of the sounds of the men's drunken snoring, the beer cans, the dirty washing they insisted on leaving behind. Jo did not seem to mind, but it finally came to a head, beginning in the small restaurant they fancied, through the biting words at Kimball's, while a trio of locals—a man and two women who also frequented the bar—looked on inscrutably, to Stan's drunken fumbling on the beach where the he and Bill had insisted they go. And where Stan had wandered away, stooping over Jo while Bill had flopped down beside her, his body partially over hers, breathed beerily into her face and mumbled that "we're all 'avin' a bit of a change, like." She was no prude, had even known that this was a possibility, even fancied Bill: a whipcord mustachioed broker from Perth. But the drunken pawing had not lived up to her image of what she wanted. She had pushed away from Bill, shoved him roughly into the sand when he had protested, and stalked off brushing sand from her shorts and halter. The sight of the three locals from Kimball's, their arms around each other, watching her coolly as she brushed by them in her disheveled state, had not helped any. And she had refused Jo entrance to the room until she had been convinced she was without the men, who, it turned out, had gone back to Kimball's for another beer.

Just now she could hear Jo's breathing from the other bed. She looked at her watch. It was three o'clock. A sliver of moon was giving some light. The hotel room was suddenly unbearable. She groped in the dark for some clothes, found her halter, smelling faintly of beer and strongly of her sweat, and her ragged shorts, kicking her sodden panties aside.

She walked out on the beach. The town lights were dim, and she had the sea, it's phosphorescent sparks, the sound of the waves, to herself. She walked away, her toes sinking into the crisp sand. To her left rose the perfect cone and peaks of Mt. Meru, hidden by palms and bushes. Stars twinkled overhead, staring down at

Tau'tevu

her without mercy or compassion. She had read somewhere of the Polynesian gods, fearful beings, animal headed, fierce—and shivered only half in jest—it was a night for all of them to be out.

As she thought that, the sounds that had accompanied her for some time forced themselves into her consciousness. There were footsteps in the sand other than her own. She turned, half in annoyance, knowing it was probably Stan, back from the boozer, or else Jo, intent in her bumbling way on "helping" her.

Behind her, half seen in the dark, almost treading in her footsteps, loomed a man. She stared for a second, shocked into immobility. He said nothing, allowing her for a long moment to examine him in the poor light. His hair was decorated with red flowers. A necklace of teeth hung in loops over his broad chest. Around his hips was twisted a rattan belt in intricate knots. One hand held a *'pa*,—a wooden sword, like the one she had seen at the local museum—at his side. The vicious sharks' teeth embedded in its edge glittered in the starlight. The other hand was reaching for her with steady deliberation. A bracelet of obsidian and shells chimed on the hard wrist. He was naked, and the massive erection swaying before his belly left no room for speculation about his intentions.

She gasped, and even without giving herself breath or time to scream, ran down the beach. The pounding of his feet followed. Sara ran wildly, and she was in excellent condition. Nonetheless, the sand sucked at her feet and slowed her down. And the pursuing figure behind her ran on without slowing. She tried running on the packed sand left by retreating waves, and that speeded her up a bit, but the man's pace never slackened, and all the time she was conscious of the blunt club jutting from his loins that pierced the air before him. Her breath coming in sobs, she raised her eyes in the hope of seeing someone, something, that would help her. A female figure, outlined by the moonlight, was running toward her.

"Here!" Sara cried. "Help! Help me!" and she turned and ran through the sand toward the approaching woman. She slowed as she got closer. The woman, her frizzy hair worn in a great afro, was naked too, and when she turned her face, Sara's heart sank. Her face was painted in black and brown swirls, giant fangs painted over her lips and chin.

"Oh no, oh nooo!" Sara spun on her heels, there was nowhere to go but toward the sea, and she leaped for the waves. The other two charged after her. She stomped her way into the water, the tiny wavelets of the lagoon snagging playfully at her ankles, then when she was about to go thigh deep, with her pursuers splashing behind her, she saw a third figure rising from the waves. This one too was female, with a face out of a nightmare. It was red and blue, huge white eyeballs gleaming in black circles.

"No, no…please. Please don't." Like a doe at bay, Sara fell to her knees in the mild surf, encircled by her pursuers. Rough uncaring hands caught her shoulders and hands and she was rolled in the water, then hauled out to the beach.

"Please don't," she panted. "Please. I'll give you money, anything, please don't…."

She was thrown onto the sand and began trembling, expecting…in a calm, almost icy corner of her mind she realized suddenly that she was not afraid of being raped. It was the irrational fear of ceasing, of being killed that was paramount, but under that, under that was a black pool of discontent with her life and of its sameness, that made her almost suicidal. Instead of throwing themselves on her, her three captors merely ranged themselves around her, watching. Her cries diminished as she realized that besides the man's club, there were no weapons in sight, and, in fact, none of her captors were actually doing anything. The painted or tattooed faces looked down on her impassively. The male's huge phallus jutted out, glistening in the wan light. The woman in the afro massaged her breasts, pinching her own nipples with power and assurance. The slimmer woman, whose dark smooth hair fell to her waist, had her hand stuck between her legs, while the other was behind her.

Her fright rapidly diminishing, Sara watched her captors watching her. The *kanak* woman turned from her, and bent forward, her full breasts edging toward her chin, her strong thigh muscles and powerful ass etched strongly in the faint light. She crab-walked backwards to the male, forcing his erection deep into herself without a perceptible change of expression. Her hips gyrated and her soft rear mounds made sucking sounds against the man's belly. She pulled forward and rose, her frightening countenance looking down at a stunned Sara.

The other woman stepped forward and Sara shrank back. With an arrogantly dismissive movement of her shoulder, the slim figure stepped toward the man. Her arms went around his neck. One leg rose high in the air, snaking between the bodies to rest on the man's shoulder. Sara could see the length of a shaven cunt, the black anal bud twisted to a slit by the woman's stance. She contorted her hips in a sudden movement, and the long male shaft plunged into her body. For a second she stood there, only her hips moving in tiny shivers, then she climbed off and stood back.

The three of them moved away from Sara at a word of command, and they stood in a line, their painted faces examining Sara with no visible emotion. The way for her to go back to the town and the hotel was open.

Sara licked her lips nervously and rose to her feet. She looked at them carefully, and backed away, then turned to run. They made no move to follow, and suddenly she felt she was being ridiculous. Her running dropped to a slow walk. She looked nervously over her shoulder. The three of them were still standing in a line, but the man was turning away from her in dismissal, turning toward the sea. The heavy woman was the only one to spare her a glance, her face a smear in the light.

Sara suddenly felt like a fool. There was a void, a gap, a hunger in the pit of her belly where previously there had been nothing but fear. Her footsteps slowed. She was panting now, not from fear or exertion, but from a feeling of aching want, something she had never felt before. Almost without any will on her part she found herself turning again, heading back to the small group. Her palms were moist with sweat. She felt as she had on her first serious date, knowing she was going to go all the way, not sure how to convey it. The three were standing together in a group, the man idly stroking one woman, the other's hand resting casually on his erect penis, in a posture so sure, so certain of ownership and belonging, that Sara's heart ached with desire. She angled her path to pass in front of them, and they ignored her, excluded her from their company by their stance. She turned her face as she passed within a couple of feet, seeking for some recognition in their faces. Just then, the moon which had been hidden by a wisp of cloud came out, shining wanly on the man's face. A mask out of nightmare in swirls of color, black and white in the dim light, stared back at her. Involuntarily she shrieked, and then, realizing what she must do, she cried out again, and began running away from the twinkling lights of the town.

She was conscious of feet pounding in pursuit. She expected to be caught quickly. Instead, the three figures hounded her down the beach, never actually catching her, though fingers raked her flanks, and something fast and painful slashed at her back and shoulders. She ran on and on, weeping and calling in fear. A stitch in her side caused her to stumble suddenly, and before she could catch her stride, the three of them were upon her.

She flailed at them, as hard as she could, to no avail. Hands slapped at her anatomy, tearing at her clothes until she was completely naked. A rough hand grabbed her hair and her neck was pulled upwards as she was pulled to the sand. Lips were applied to her mouth, sucking at her tongue which fluttered like a frightened bird. Sara tried to scream but the imprisoning mouth denied her this freedom. The lips withdrew, and she was pushed and prodded to one of the nearby coconut palms. The bark was rough against her back, her bottom, the tops of her thighs, and finally her arms as she was bound securely to the upright growth. Her ankles were tied on either side of the trunk, feet digging into the loam at the base.

The man leaned forward, his nightmare face only a dim shadow in the dark. His face occluded the moon and he kissed Sara with a passion she had never felt before. His long and mobile tongue explored her mouth, fluttered against her tongue and palate, dipped almost to her throat. Sara reveled in the touch, pushed her chest forward in mute request. His hands were soon on her full breasts, playing with her nipples, squeezing the breasts with firm purpose. Sara wriggled and found herself conscious of the rough bark. With writhing movements she rubbed herself against the bark, a roughness that sent signals of wished-for pleasure to her brain even through the abrasions of her skin.

Another mouth applied itself to the space between her legs, and Sara felt a great sensation of peace and joy. She knew she liked women, had always liked women, but this was the first time she had ever experienced what she had secretly longed for. She thrust her mound hard against the top of the head she could not see, and a moist tongue trailed its way up the insides of her thighs, leaving a slick trail that headed, inevitably, for the nest of golden curls at the juncture of her thighs and lower belly. Breathless, barely responding to the demands of the male mouth on her own, she waited for the arrival of the anticipated touch.

The mouth touched the crack between her legs and Sara cried out aloud in desire and triumph. The man hummed in his throat and pushed against her, and she rewarded his patience with a duet of lingual caresses that stimulated them both. She rubbed her ass in circular motions against the trunk, then pushed her hips forward to meet the demanding female lips at her mound. She knew she was dripping wet, and the expert lips began sipping at her dew, licking deep into the recess, teasing her clitoris for more and more of her honey.

The female head at her crotch pushed forcefully forward, and a finger insinuated itself between her buttocks, to the tiny button of her anus. Sara pushed hard back, then slumped, allowing the force to push her roughly against the scraping bark. She cried out into the encompassing face glued to hers, and he increased the tempo and force of his hands at her breast.

Sara was now in a complete trance. She pushed herself back onto the imprisoning trunk, accepting the abrading of the welcoming bark. The tongue at the juncture of her legs pushed deeply into her cunt, the finger worked its way into her backside. Sara exulted in the pain these actions brought. They revived her skin, made it tingle and demand more, and, for now, she could see the shining mountain of the true grail, the true orgasm she had sought for fruitlessly for so long. Her body quivered in the beginnings of an orgasm, and she thrust herself, gave herself fully, to the sensations of the moment. Shudders raged in her body, sending shock waves even up the trunk of the stolid palm.

When she cried out in a frenzy of delight, the heads withdrew from her body.

"OOOahhhhh. Oh God! Oh yes, again! Please, again." There were tears of desire and lust in her eyes, and some rational corner of her mind could not believe she had actually said that. She opened her eyes to see that the man and woman had withdrawn slightly from her.

"Please," she begged. "Again. I must have you again…"

The words died in her throat. The slim figure in the blue face paint stepped closer. She ran a long stream of separate lashes through her fingers. Sara's breath caught in her throat. She had never understood people like that...people who...she could barely think of the term. Now, suddenly, it was a terrifying reality, and her fears returned. She shrank from the lash-carrying figure. It was the solid bole of the palm against which she was tied that brought her back to herself. The roughness of the bark once again abraded her ass, and the crackle of pain and electricity that it generated brought back a better understanding of herself. She straightened her torso, waiting expectantly.

The thin leather streamers were brought down almost casually against the skin of her belly. It burned a path of fire onto her skin from side to side. She screamed, a high ululating cry of shock "Nooooo!" But before the call could reach its full volume, a mouth was on hers, absorbing the sound.

She panted, shaking, wondering whether she could bear the second blow she knew must come. The thin figure raised the lash almost lazily, her long dark hair blowing strands over her shoulder. The pain was no more bearable this time, except that another sensation seemed to filter its rawness. Sara felt a glow rise from her exposed and wet cunt to meet the fiery glow from the lash. This time she did not bother screaming, knowing how useless it was. More strokes followed and the lash rose gradually, manipulated by the thin expert hands, to strike her breasts, then down over her belly until they stroked the heat in her loins to unbearable proportions.

The lash dropped to the sand, and the slim figure entwined herself sinuously around Sara's bound form.

Delicate lips sought her own, and the girl, smelling faintly of sandalwood, murmured, "You were wonderful."

Her entire torso smarting, and her insides glowing in lust, Sara could only close her eyes and return the passionate kiss. Her hips were gyrating on their own, completely out of control as she sought the relief of contact. When she opened her eyes she found the other woman standing by her side. She held a flexible wand ending in a flat hand-shaped small paddle. She pulled Sara's mouth to hers, and her tongue darted deeply into Sara's demanding mouth.

"That's so good. Please, again," Sara begged as the kiss ended. Instead the woman raised her hand and lashed the paddle end against Sara's exposed cunt.

"No! Not there!" Sara cried in momentary panic. Once again her objections were stilled as the other applied her mouth. The slap slap of the paddle against Sara's well-padded pussy drowned out her muffled cries.

Another orgasm built up in Sara's frame, and the pain in her cunt fanned it to epic proportions. She shuddered once again, then slumped almost senseless from her bonds.

The three figures stood away from her. The man said something in a low voice, and the larger of the two women stepped behind the palm tree and Sara felt her bonds fall free. Then they stood before her, perfectly poised, watching her expressionlessly.

For a second Sara thought that was all there was, then she understood what they were offering. In a frenzy of excitement she fell on the three passive figures. She ran her fingers over their bare skins, exploring their cavities, touching and fondling without let. She rubbed herself furiously against the man, and when that was not enough, she tried to force herself onto his massive erection first covering it with her mouth, then trying clumsily to mount him.

"You bloody bastard," she breathed in frustration. "I want your goddamn cock inside me. These bitches only warmed me up. Fuck you...no, fuck me!" she was almost screaming at the silent immobile figures, though they followed each of her moves with their eyes. She raced back to the palm and found the lash, slashing about at the figures wildly, cursing.

"Come on, you pommy cock. Do *something!*" she was weeping in frustration, and the lash dropped nervelessly from her hand. Slowly she fell to her knees before the three of them.

"Please, please master. I beg of you!" the words welled out of some deep hidden pool. "Please. Help me, master, boss I need it so badly...."

He was on her in a flash. The two women, moving in accord, parted her knees. Sara was pushed back in the sand and he crouched between her legs. She guided his massive shaft into her wet entrance, crying out as the broad head parted her lips and sank into her golden fuzz. The sand formed a pleasant, gritty irritant as he forced his shaft deeper into her. His powerful ass muscles rammed his shaft deeply into her waiting cunt. The roughness of his thrust tensed her muscles and her nerves responded with signals of pure pleasure that made her dig her heels into the yielding sand, then raise them to clench over the muscular moving back. His hands gouged at her ass muscles, his mouth sought hers and the full weight of his body ground her abraded back into the sand.

"Oh.... Oh God.... Oh yes. Please fuck me. Fuck, fuck. Oaaahhh," Sara's cries were demented, almost mad in their intensity as the surge of her orgasm lifted both their frames above the sand and he continued boring into her. She collapsed, her muscles like jelly, and was only barely conscious of the thrusting pump of his cock as it pulsed his white cream into every fold of her cunt.

When he finished, he brought her sandy fingers to her cunt. Forcing her fingers in, she could feel the thick globules of his residue. She resisted weakly, but was too exhausted to do much, and the soothing gritty feel of her own fingers forced to rub her cunt hairs allayed her resistance. He rose from her body, and Sara found herself shadowed by one of the women whose broad shoulders blocked out the crescent moon.

The woman threw herself onto the supine white body like an eagle stooping. There was no time for Sara to react. She had often thought of making love to a woman, but never like this. In her imaginings it was always a slow, delicious, delicate approach, something romantic with candlelight. The *kanak* woman had obviously never intended any romance. Her mouth, smelling faintly of pandanus was forced onto Sara's. She ground her hips ferociously against the Australian's, and rubbed her breasts in great slapping movements against the pinkness beneath her. Sara was too surprised to cry out against this violation at first. Then, when she had gathered her wits, she found that the rough grainy friction of the other woman's mound against her own was bringing on an unexpected reaction. Unconsciously, she discovered, her hips were playing her outraged feelings traitor, and were responding to their rough treatment.

Curiosity overtook her, and in a daring experiment, she thrust her tongue deeply through the other woman's lips. Throughout the furious battering on her mound, she found the delicacy she had expected, as the *kanak*'s tongue responded to her own with a delicate game of hide-and-seek. And yet, she found, when the woman on top of her slowed her furious hip pounding, that she wanted, ached, for that violent contact. Her hands reached out, covered as they were with a mud of golden sand and come, and raked the other woman's flanks viciously. The *kanak* responded with a cry, and her own palms, hard, strong, slapped viciously against Sara's exposed thighs.

"Slave! Captive slave!" the *kanak* called out in English. "Give me pleasure. Give what you have. The chief has had you but now you are mine!"

Sara responded to these cries and found herself enslaved in reality. The demanding woman above her *was* her mistress. She would have to do whatever was needed to satisfy her. She was alone in this savage land, far from help, and to avoid more punishment, she moved her body as her mistress dictated, her loins and lips clutching hungrily at the demanding body above her.

They came together in a volcanic, rolling climax that showered sand all around them, and which sapped the last of Sara's strength. The mutual orgasm wound down, and Sara found herself lying limply on the other woman. The man raised her to her feet, and together the three of them headed for the water. Sara looked around for the third of her owners, the slim woman, but she had vanished as mysteriously as she had come.

The sea was magical. There was no moon and the

luminescence of millions of sea animals made greenish streaks in the water. For a moment she feared for sharks and other bogeys of the deep, but the steady movements of her companions convinced her there was nothing to fear. They turned and swam back to the beach, emerging, all three of them, like gods of the sea. At the water's edge, without any bidding, Sara fell to her knees. Her hand reached out in the dark and found the woman's smooth thighs. She offered her mouth wordlessly, and the other moved closer, parting her thighs and straddling Sara's uplifted face. The first taste was salty, tasting of sea and fresh life. Then the natural flavors of the woman's sex surged through, and Sara's mouth was flooded with the warm earthy taste of womanhood. She drank deeply, her tongue laving every crease and fold. It was a wordless farewell. She rose to go without a word, without looking back, and did not hear the parting footsteps of her two anonymous lovers in the sand as they walked away from her.

Back at the room, Sara slipped quietly into the bathroom. She showered luxuriously. Jo, in the other bed, stirred in her sleep at the sound but did not wake. There was still some sand in the folds of her pussy, and she hunted it out, scraping with a finger which sent a thrill of secondary climax through her frame. She examined her bruises and scrapes in the tiny bathroom mirror. Smiling in reverie, wrapped in a large woolly towel, she crept back in the pre-dawn dimness to her bed. There was enough light to see that the covers had fallen off Jo. For a lengthy moment Sara looked with carefully hidden lust at her friend. Jo's dark triangle of hair was halfway exposed. Her thigh, still pale after a week in the sun, was a long clean line leading to a smooth haunch and rounded ass. She snored lightly, ladylike, and Sara imagined herself kissing the red budded mouth. When Jo stirred in her sleep, Sara climbed back into bed. Her last thought was to wonder whether Jo would taste like the *kanak* woman, whose name she would never know.

Chapter 11

There had been several brief squalls that afternoon, and the beach still smelled of rain. There was a restlessness in Sara's groin, a demand for something she knew she could not have. When Jo suggested they go out that evening as they usually did, Sara refused, and after a long puzzled glance, Jo had gone off by herself. Restless, Sara had put on brightly printed muumuu of the kind sold to tourists, and wandered onto the dark beach.

She stood looking out to sea, well past the beaches normally frequented by tourists, not far, in her estimate, from the events of the previous night, when she felt a movement on the sand by her. She glanced to her side expectantly, then slumped in disappointment. It was only a slim Indian girl dressed in slacks and blouse, beautiful like hundreds Sara had seen on the island, her luminous eyes bright in the reflected light of the hotel area and the moon. The girl kept coming, then made a quick movement. Sara felt a stiff noose tighten about her neck. Her first urge was to run, then relief, fear, anticipation and lust surged through her frame in a mass of churning emotions. She raised her hand slowly and felt the noose, that had been tightened but not to the point of choking. It was woven of smooth rattan, flexible and tough. There was a tug on it, and she followed the Indian girl as she led her wordlessly across the beach.

They came to a fence behind which Sara recognized the large hut that had harbored her the previous night. Obediently, she followed the lead. The Indian girl did something to the other end, and Sara found herself tethered like a dog to the porch railing. Then slim, busy hands were upon her and her dress was ripped from her shoulders and dropped to the sand. She tried to look around, and could barely see the slim figure of her tormentor disappear into the dark doorway. Alone and naked, she waited as goose pimples rose on her body.

Some time later, minutes, hours, she could not tell, two female figures came for her. She was led into the native house, her heart pounding, her skin pimpled by the cold and anticipation. As they led her, the two women did not exchange a word, but their hands twitched and their eyes were upon her in brief periods, as if they could not wait to get their hands on her, but had been forbidden to do so. The walk through the house was brief, but Sara could feel her throat constrict, and her vaginal canal, which had been dry, moistened with anticipation. She was conscious of the lips of her cunt sliding wetly against each other with every frightened yet anticipating stride she took.

She found herself in a grass-walled room. The dried herbage rustled with the wind, but otherwise muffled every sound. The wooden floor was covered with the thick woven rush mats of Tau'tevu. There was no ceiling, and from naked beams hung unidentifiable bundles, wooden masks, bamboo containers and implements. The three of them stood together before the thick woven mat, decorated in rich patterns, that covered the center of the hut. On it lay a man. His head rested on an elaborately carved wooden headrest. He was naked but for a necklace of bright shells. Resting on his muscular stomach lay lengths of colored rattan which he was braiding with sure fingers. They waited patiently for him to notice them. Finally Sara's lover of the previous night raised his head. Dark fathomless eyes stared deeply into her own. His fingers stilled and he held up an object for their inspection. It was a short, rather stiff whip of braid, ending in a flexible tassel of some material Sara did not recognize. He looked at her steadily, and she knew that a flush of anticipation and longing was rising from her loins to her breasts, and finally reached her face.

He offered her the whip. Sara stood quite still. Her breathing was turning to a rapid panting, and she knew that she had to make a decision. The other three waited in silence for her to make up her mind. Tentatively, she knelt on the mat, trying to emulate the grace of the island women she had seen. She crept forward over the rustling material and took the whip, then crept back. She put the whip in the *kanak* woman's hand, then deliberately turned her back. Conscious of the man's scrutiny, she bent forward until her hair brushed the floor.

"Beat me," she said simply. "I've needed it for a long time. Beat me hard. Use me. Fuck me!" The last was a wail of unsatisfied lust. She peered back between her legs at Orpheo, holding herself rigid with an effort. The dark woman knelt by her side until their faces were a handbreadth apart. Deliberately she grasped Sara's blonde hair in her fist. She raised the whip just as slowly. At the apex of her swing she held her position for a moment, then brought the whip down blindingly fast onto Sara's exposed buttocks.

"Ooooh shit!"

Sara's bum simply refused to register the blow for the first brief moment. It was as if she had been struck by a snake. The pain spread from her spongy gluteus along her spine. She rocked forward on her feet, and would have fallen but for the hand tangled in her hair. A wild, uncontrolled scream erupted from her mouth which she muffled in a cut off snorting sound. Now her ass registered the blow as a line of fire which extended crosswise over her buttocks.

Sara's tormentor rose and handed the whip to the darker, Indian girl. She turned toward Sara, grasped her hair, and hauled her to her feet. The picture of the small Indian woman holding Sara's larger paler frame erect by the hair would have made Sara laugh but for the terrible certainty of the whip wielder. The Indian twisted her hand more tightly into Sara's hair, and turned her around to face the man on the cushion. Her head held immobile, Sara examined the man. His prick, which had been flaccid before, and lay along his thigh, was noticeably thicker. It had rolled onto his stomach, exposing his balls fully to her gaze, and she knew that as she watched it would thicken and harden.

With Sara still facing the man, the Indian girl raised her hand with the whip.

Though she had experienced the blow before, and though she knew what to expect, this whip stroke was no easier than the first. The massive blow from the instrument sent her hips forward in an instinctive attempt to avoid the pain. At the back of her mind Sara knew that her stance enhanced the view of her cunt, and she felt her juices quicken. But the fire and the pain, the pain that ran up her spine to her skull, brought another scream to her throat, and this time she did not attempt to control it. As she yelled, she saw, with satisfaction, through the red mist of pain, that the cock was hardening, standing well above the flat muscles of the man's stomach.

"Let her have it!" The man's voice was a clear tenor, commanding and vibrant. "She knows her body best."

Both women stood away. The one with the whip handed it to Sara. For a second she regretted the command. She wanted to do what *he* wanted, and then she suddenly realized that being beaten was the easier choice. Now she would really have to prove her own ability. She raised the whip. The handle was heavier, the braiding more dense, and it was shaped like a crude, knobby, cock. Holding it firmly, her eyes intently on the male figure before her, Sara brought the whip down hard across her full white breasts. "Mmmmm!" she screamed with her lips clenched, then again "Mmmmaaaa!" as she struck again, then again. With each blow the cock in front of her hardened and thickened until she found herself in a frenzy of excitation, her breasts and buttocks lacerated by the blows of the whip. Now, almost losing control, intent only on pleasing the enigmatic figure before her, she reversed the whip. Spreading her legs, she opened her slicked cunt with one hand, then rammed the whip handle into herself. The relief was unbearable and she jerked the objects several times against her swollen clitoris crying out in pleasure mixed with pain as the weave caught the folds of her cunt and pinched them to a deeper red. Trembling uncontrollably now, she spun around and crouched on the mat before him, her buttocks high in the air. She pulled her ass cheeks apart with one hand, then rammed the stiff cock-handle into her tight rectal entrance. The pain of the penetration almost stopped her, but it was his command that forced her to her senses.

"Look!" he said, and Sara immediately ceased, obedient to his wishes, and spun around, still kneeling, to face him.

The two women held the tumescence up for her inspection. One of them held up something else. A ring edged with sharp projections, something like a tiny crown. She slipped this over the erect cock until it merged with the dark hairs at the base.

"Come here," he said, and Sara shivered again.

Sara crouched over his proffered body, spreading her knees wide, then reaching beneath her to part the lips of her cunt, widening the hole between them. Deliberately, slowly, she lowered herself onto the massive member, the head nosing into her receptacle, followed by the shaft until she could feel the pinpricks of the band around the base. She looked into his eyes, her own wide and questioning, then she suddenly relaxed her thigh muscles, allowing her body weight to carry her downwards, onto the sharp projections. She struggled to contain her shriek unsuccessfully as the tiny pinpoints bit into the inflamed tender tissues of her inner lips. The struggle to control her reflex to rise from the fiery touch was tougher, but she managed to control her urge to flee, though her thigh muscles trembled and her forehead beaded with sweat. The man looked up at her impassively, though there was the hint of approval in the set of his face. The women looked on, their emotions hidden.

Sara began rocking herself, embedding the points deeper into her tender flesh. With each move the pain grew deeper, but paradoxically more bearable. She moaned as she moved, her hands touching her own lacerated breasts, her stomach, pulling at her own hair. She forced herself deeper onto the cock, which became an instrument for the pleasure of her tormented and demanding flesh. She felt that she was composed only of discrete sensations that wormed their way through her frame. Crying out in abandon she raised her tit to her mouth and licked, then bit the nipple. Her hand smacked against her buttock, forcing the reluctant pudginess deeper onto the forbidding teeth that stuck into her tender parts.

As her demands grew, she suddenly recalled the whip. Groping behind her she found it where she had flung it. Her fierce gaze turned until she saw one of the other women. She pulled, her hands grasping smooth flesh, then lashed out in a fury. The woman tried to shrink away but was stopped by a wordless command from the male whose cock was inserted inside Sara's deepest recesses. Again she lashed out, and heard the slap as the stiff leather braid impacted reluctant female flesh. Her own demands were rising, and she knew she had to impose her demands quickly. The other woman was there, and Sara lashed out, flailing wildly until she connected. Her other hand grasped her own breast, squeezing brutally, sending a message of pain and pleasure to her hindbrain. When some of the wildness had been let out, she opened her eyes. Reversing the whip she handed it to the *kanak* woman, then bent forward onto the waiting man's chest. The prickles welcomed her, and the expected lash of the whip struck her in the crack of her buttocks like a loving welcome. She screamed once again, fire rising in her skin along with waves of sexual heat. The woman behind her set to work to lash her and Sara rocked herself with each blow, trying to drive the crown of thorns deeper into her ravaged cuntal tissues.

She raised her head. The Indian woman was crouched over the man's face, proffering herself to his tongue. Sara reached out and gathered the slim figure to her. She sat erect, and brought the woman onto her lap.

Padmini twined herself around the hips of the blonde on Orpheo's cock. The tourist's eyes were glaring, and she was forcing herself deeper onto the male member. Sliding sinuously, Padmini forced the woman's broad hips onto the male member, whilst behind the tourist, Vivian lashed away, her free hand inserted into her own cunt.

They came together in a rocking, thundering climax. Orpheo's massive cock erupted a white froth into Sara's thirsty orifice. She cried out, a wild, high cry of complete release, and stiffened as she felt, for the first time in her life, the cuntal constriction of a complete orgasm. Hardly knowing what she was doing she curled her hands into claws and raked at the male chest under her, forcing the pleasure pricking sensations of maleness deeper into her soft insides. Then she collapsed forwards, her breasts mashing against the man's hard pectoral muscles.

They were roused by the sound of crockery. Wordlessly, as they disentangled themselves, Vivian handed each of the others a mug of hot tea. The drink was so prosaic Sara wanted to laugh, and when the Indian girl turned to her and said, "How do you do, I am Padmini," in cultured tones, her happiness at the absurdity was complete.

Chapter 12

Sara walked down the lane, conscious of the smells around her. Cooking of fish and coconut milk. Pandanus flowers. The ubiquitous smell of *kava*. Chickens. People passed her. Tourists and locals out for a stroll. Bicycles whispered by with occasional soft greeting emanating from their riders or passers-by.

Then the sound of a car. One of the small island jeepneys. She walked on, ignoring it, knowing the island drivers inevitably sounded their horns when they approached pedestrians. The sound of the jeepney did not vary however. She peered over her shoulder. The face of the driver was familiar.

It was Padmini's face. But of a masculine cast. The finely boned features were covered by dark smooth skin. He was watching her stolidly through tinted lenses that hid some of his expression. She turned aside, waiting for the car to pass. Instead he slowed down, matching her walk. Waiting.

For a long moment she was nonplused. Afraid? No, not after the previous night, merely wondering. Then in a flash she knew what she had to do. She climbed into the jeepney and it accelerated away smoothly, unlike most island cars which roared sootily and complained of poor maintenance. The man, nameless, looked at her, then at a bundle that lay between the front seats. He did not say a word. She opened the cloth. Inside was a dyed fabric wraparound, a necklace made of shark's teeth interspersed with coral and carved beads, and a second, double loop of the same make. In the light of a passing car she could see the wraparound was made of richly woven grass textile—an art peculiar to Tau'tevu. The cloth must be worth a fortune, she thought as she caressed it wonderingly.

"Now," the man said, breaking into her thoughts. "*He* says now."

"What do you mean 'now'?"

He looked straight ahead, declining to answer. Letting her figure it out by herself. The jeepney was traveling slowly, as if giving her the opportunity to leave. They reached a crossroads. Turning one way would bring her back to the town, back to the hotel. Turning the other...

The driver slowed down, almost came to a stop, obviously waiting for her decision. Her palms were sweaty, and her breathing harsh in her ears. For a moment she wanted to ask him to direct the car back to the safety of the hotel and her own kind. Then she suddenly realized what she was thinking. Own kind? Where there any such? And if so, what were they? Who were they? Her mind's eye saw the tourists, sprawled in their beds or café chairs.

Without answering, knowing she need say nothing, she took out the necklace and hung it around her neck. The teeth pinked her skin lightly, threatening and welcoming at once. The sensitive nerves in the swimming muscles where her back met her neck were touched lightly. The lower part of the strand caught in the fabric of the blouse over her breasts. The driver looked on approvingly, his dark Indian face almost immobile, then he let in the clutch and drifted down the road.

"Now," he repeated.

She nodded, knowing, then in the dark, with the Indian's eyes on the road, she slipped out of her clothes, dropping them in a heap on the back seat of the jeepney. Squirming around, she wrapped herself in the fabric. She thought for a moment of baring her breasts, using it merely as a sarong, then remembered the second necklace. She slid it up her legs. The larger loop went around her belly, the smaller around her thigh. The joint rested on her hip. The sharp lines dug into the flesh of her thigh and back as she settled into the seat. At first she gasped, then the sensation started her nerves to firing and she settled back, expectant yet relaxed, the cloth bound about her from barely-covered nipples to upper thigh. The driver turned and smiled at her, white teeth glinting approvingly in the dark face.

The jeep stopped before the fence that enclosed the house on Taualea Point. This time the entrance was clearly lit by a lamp that shed a cheerful glow on the beds of flowers that lined the walk and crowded on the porch. They walked side by side, the blonde woman and the dark thin handsome man went up to the door and he ushered her in. Once again she was taken to the rush-mat floored room, to face Orpheo, Padmini, and Vivian.

The three of them looked at her in approval. They too wore nothing but flower *lei* and sarongs. Padmini's was diaphanous, showing her slim girlish body and the hairless mound. Vivian's in vivid black, brown, and white colors, had been cut through in an intricate pattern that showed her brown flesh as she moved. Radh joined them, dressed in nothing but a wreath of flowers. He approached Sara from behind, seizing her wrists in his hands and bending her arms backwards in a grip that she could not resist. Gradually her back curved until she was staring upwards, into his demanding face. His lips descended onto hers and covered her mouth, invading her oral cavity with undeniable force. Other hands than his stripped her sarong off, and another demanding mouth was fastened to her cunt, sending shivers of pleasure into her belly. Another unseen mouth fastened on her breast, the teeth working their way into the sensitive nubbin of her nipple. The mouth at her groin was replaced by bunched fingers which forced their way painfully up into her channel, moistening the tissues as they went. The scent of vanilla oil spread through the room and a pleasant sting started in her crotch.

The pressure on her arms pulled her backwards and she let herself fall, trusting in her lovers. They lowered her down onto her back, and she could finally see the rest of the room.

Orpheo stood before her in all his naked glory, his

cock at half mast, the muscles under his smooth skin bulging unconsciously. Her legs held spread open by the man and the woman, Sara watched him in the torch light over the pink-tipped mounds of her breasts, conscious of the open inviting furry mouth she presented to him. Her pulse was pounding loudly in her veins, and the arch of her lower back kept the feel of the waist band to a mere prickle.

Vivian emerged from the gloom. She was naked but for the print wraparound skirt in black and brown patterns that swirled around her thighs and calves. Her nipples, erect over her full brown mounds, were black in the semi-dark, peering at Sara blindly. She knelt before the man and engulfed the length of his cock in her mouth until Sara could see the bulge in Vivian's throat, and the thick lips nuzzled the bush of crisp hair. Vivian moved her head backwards until the glistening shaft showed its full length. Then she rounded her lips and pulled the head in, licking it fiercely.

She started a fucking motion with her head, dancing to an unheard melody, twisting her head sideways and up and down, forcing the length deeper into it. Her cheeks bulged from time to time with her movement, as the shaft became harder, longer, more demanding. The man's eyes remained focused on the split between Sara's legs, and she found herself blushing, to her amazement.

Finally Vivian withdrew her head. Reluctantly, the tip popped out of her mouth, now fully erect. Vivian fumbled beside her in the dark and produced two long strips. They glittered dully in the light. Padmini left Sara's side and knelt beside Vivian. The two women worked rapidly to weave the moist-seeming straps around the erect member before them. Without rising, they moved aside and he took one step forward, standing between Sara's spread thighs.

She looked at the sight in horror. From the thicket between his legs his manhood stood monstrously jutting into the air. The straps were made of the skin of a guitar fish, polished so that the small platelets and knobs that covered the ray-like creatures skin stood out in a pattern of tiny white knobs. The tightness of the weave made his cock bulge in small folds, and the head was a flaming red, looking like that of a man strangled. Or in great passion.

He allowed her to look at the apparition to her satisfaction. She knew she could, she should, rise and flee. They would not stop her now. She moved uncomfortably and the sharp teeth bit into her side, bringing her back to her senses and desires. She fell back softly, passively. He fell forward, precipitating himself onto her willing soft body. The contact forced the breath from her lungs. Then the monstrous head was at her swampy wet opening, fumbling for a brief second. He tensed the muscles of his back, then thrust forward brutally, without any preparation.

Sara screamed. She knew she should scream. The knobs of the straps tore at the sensitive membranes of her vulva. It was a smooth sensation, as if someone had run a string of pearls across her soul. The worst was not the knobs—it was the monumental, uncaring power and size of his thrust which reached to her welcoming womb. Stunned, she lay there as he pulled back, then smashed into her again, their hairs melding wetly.

He arched his body over hers abruptly. Now his body was completely unsupported except where it came into contact with hers. His feet and the upper part of his torso were in the air, their loins joined fiercely, and Sara screamed once again as the teeth in her waist and thigh bands, which had been nothing more than pinpricks to that point, drove into her flesh. Instinctively she knew what to do. Her knees rose to surround the man's hams. Her hand dug roughly into the hard muscles of his buttocks, and she began rocking herself and her man to ecstasy.

Chapter 13

Sara arched her back. Vivian stood behind her, contemplating the gift of rounded pale moons. To the side Orpheo sat cross-legged, his face impassive. Padmini was twined around him, her neck arched back in pleasure, her hands and hips in constant motion. Sara peered at them through the lanky locks of her dark blonde hair. Her face showed her longing, her desire to replace Padmini.

Vivian nudged the rounded thigh with a hard toe. Her hands dropped to the basket-weave table and came up with a hard object, straps dangled from it, and Sara's breath caught in her throat, her rear muscles tensing. Vivian brooded behind her.

The *kanak* girl dropped her skirt. Her full dark bush sprang into view, the dark lips hidden between her muscular thighs. With quick moves she ran the straps around her hips. She nudged Sara urgently again as she did so, and Sara turned her face in time to catch a large masculine-seeming object rise above the darker woman's thighs. Before she had time to react Vivian had fallen to her knees, parting Sara's calves with a rough hand. One hand gripped the artificial cock firmly. The other strong hand clasped the Australian girl's fleshy hip. With undeniable purpose Vivian placed the rounded head of the cock at Sara's wet cunt, moving it back and forth on the lips briefly while she searched for the entrance.

With one smooth move she rose to her feet to crouch over Sara's proffered hips, then sank deeply forward with a savage cry.

Vivian's call of pleasure and triumph was echoed by Sara as the massive vibrator sank deeply into her flesh. It was immense, the largest object she had ever had in her cunt. Though she had been expecting the insertion, she had not expected the power of the *kanak* girl's thrust, nor the rapid bucking that followed. She felt as if the brown girl hated her, so rough and deep were her thrusts. Sara tried to struggle, tried to accommodate herself in some way to the moves, and found herself imprisoned by Vivian's implacable strength. Sara cried out again and turned her face to remonstrate with Vivian. The *kanak*'s warm breath was on her face. Vivian's heavy demanding mouth was on her own, and the *kanak*'s tongue was thrust deeply into Sara's mouth, searching out the intimate places she reserved for herself, and now for Orpheo. Vivian's hands were on her body, pinching, feeling. They moved from Sara's bruised and sensitive clitoris, to twist at her prominent and hard nipples, then to slap at her buttocks, to scratch deeply at her thighs and shoulders.

TAU'TEVU

Vivian moved again, and Sara screamed once more, this time with an unexpected rush of electric pleasure that made her frame shudder in the first of a series of climaxes. Vivian turned the vibrator up high as she plunged wildly into the pale accepting flesh before her.

Sara yelped into Vivian's exploring mouth as she felt other hands on her. She screwed her eyes around to see Padmini's dark feet at the edge of her vision. The other hands on her cunt, exploring her and Vivian's flesh indifferently, must be Orpheo's then. Sara closed her eyes and allowed sensation to flow through her. She noted dimly that something else was happening at the demanding juncture of her buttocks and Vivian's thrusting hips. For a moment the woman mounting her stopped her motion. Sara felt her buttocks parted firmly, and was not surprised to feel something hard pressed against her reluctant rectal muscles. The ring of flesh parted at the insertion, and Sara screamed again, released completely, into Vivian's mouth. She hoped dimly that the second cock was Orpheo's but the vibrating movement that joined the sound and feel of the earlier insertion dispelled that hope. She clutched at the rich woven grass mat with blunt nails, her body shuddering in pain and desire, her entire body occupied.

Orpheo finished strapping the second vibrator onto Vivian's hips and stood back to admire the picture. Sara, her face captured and obscured by Vivian's dark curls, was arching her back desperately to engulf as much of Vivian's thrusts as she could. Sweat was beading the *kanak*'s dark skin and her muscles bunched and relaxed as her hips pulsed in pleasing curves into the waiting white woman's orifices. Vivian's curl-crowned cunt was exposed and hidden in rapid motion as she plunged herself deeply and vengefully into the tourist woman.

Padmini was rolled almost into a ball. Her hands were busy, one between her legs where Orpheo's earlier discharge was being massaged wetly into her full bare quim. The other hand was clutching hungrily at Sara's rounded breasts, bringing the nipples to Padmini's demanding mouth. Each time she left off one nipple, the ring of red left by her teeth glowed brighter.

His staff was now erect once more. His eyes almost glazing, Orpheo crouched behind Vivian, then at the right moment, meeting her movement and rhythm, he inserted himself deeply into her waiting cunt. He could feel the hard slick base of Vivian's artificial cock against his scrotum. She felt his insertion, and immediately increased the force of her own thrusts. Beneath the two of them Sara groaned a muffled cry into Vivian's waiting mouth. Orpheo's hands clutched at handfuls of golden and curly black hair, guiding all their heads together.

Orpheo said something to Radh, and he emerged from the corner like an automaton. His eyes were on Padmini's demanding form on the mat. He held his cock before him like a magic wand. Thin and dark, it threatened the small girl's face. She opened her eyes wide, waiting for the insertion. Instead he knelt at Sara's head and presented himself to her mouth. Vivian made room and the long shaft was inserted into Sara's willing cavern. Sara gulped hungrily at the morsel and demanded more. Vivian licked the length of the shaft as it was inserted more deeply into the Australian girl's mouth.

At first Sara felt she would choke as the long slim cock forced its way into her mouth. But the delectation of the demanding cocks inserted in her vagina and rectum, the feeling that she was serving her master properly and painfully, and the desire to pleasure the Padmini-figure above her helped her overcome the reflex, and when, finally, the tip of the cock slid into her willing throat, it did so without a quiver.

Now she was truly impaled, helpless in the grip of her lovers, and she surrendered herself to her own pleasure. The double wreath of teeth around her thigh and hips pricked deeply into her demanding flesh with each move of the massive cocks into her holes. She knew that beads of blood were flecking her pale flesh and gloried in the pain that shot through her frame. Hands pinched and squeezed her breasts and a third cock demanded the complete obedience of her mouth while another mouth licked and kissed her cheeks and face. A volcanic eruption was starting to grow in the pit of her belly. This was the first time she had ever felt herself truly free. Her insides started convulsing, waves of pleasure emanating from the thrusts of the cock in her.

Vivian could feel the bucking of Sara's hips even through the vibrator she wore. Orpheo's persistent cock was increasing her own pleasure, and with a wild cry that was echoed by Padmini she let herself go completely, thrusting with abandon into the waiting helpless body before her. Orpheo ground his hips into her, then suddenly pulled away. He was back in a flash, showing her what he held in his hands. It was a short, braided bullwhip, and Vivian realized its import even as she approached her own climax. She pulled her upper body away from Sara, and Orpheo raised his hand.

The blow of the whip was so unexpected that it almost froze Sara in place, notwithstanding her near-orgasm. From the corner of her eye she saw the man raise the whip once again and bring it down against her upper buttocks. She screamed into Radh's cock, and in her agony, tried to bite the fleshy length. Padmini had anticipated her, however, and her thin strong fingers were holding onto Sara's jaws, keeping her from doing any damage. The next lash struck her thigh, and with the part of her mind that was not occupied with the pleasure of pain, Sara admired the man's artistry. This was what she had come to Tau'tevu for. She abandoned herself to the storm of feelings.

Orpheo stood over the knot on the floor, plying the whip with a sure and delicate hand. It flicked onto Sara, then to Vivian's thrusting buttocks, the tip striking her anal entrance and sparking pain throughout her frame. He struck again, this time at Padmini's breasts and she shuddered at the delicious pain. The lash curved around Radh's muscular thin buttocks and he thrust deeply into Sara's waiting mouth, his balls banging against her chin. With growing speed and accuracy, Orpheo conducted his symphony to its final crescendo.

Sara was a quivering mass of flesh, almost all thought pushed out of her mind by the intense pleasure of her senses. She came in a volcanic series of orgasmic eruptions that lifted her frame off the mat, bringing the others with her. Vivian convulsed with eruptions of her own, gasping and blowing as she drove herself into Sara's waiting orifices in a frenzy. Sara felt the beginning of the liquid gush from Radh flooding her throat as she collapsed onto the mat.

Radh's head was back, his throat taut. He felt the

incredible sensation of Sara's teeth encircling and digging into the base of his cock while the tip was inserted fully into the corrugations of her throat. An inescapable flood rose from his balls, and he started pumping harder into the willing woman's face, when a slim hand gripped the juncture of his balls and cock. He screamed in agony and his fury blazed up like a fire at the denial of his desires, at the pain in his privates. He looked down, the whites of his eyes reddened by the blood of his passion. Padmini was crouched at his feet, one hand between her parted legs, the other gripping him fiercely. Without thought his hand lashed out and caught her cheek. She fell backwards, sprawling on the mat, her legs parted. He saw the naked hairless gash, the pink framed by black, then by brown skin. Furiously he threw himself forward and lodged himself fully up her cunt. Pain laced his buttocks as he drove violently forward into the soft flesh toward a climax that could not be denied.

Orpheo watched Sara collapse and, at a quick nod from him, Padmini seized her brother's balls. Quickly, as Radh slapped his sister and then threw himself onto her waiting body, Orpheo grasped Sara's hair and pulled her to her feet. Vivian rolled off, the artificial cocks popping out of their receptacles in Sara's flesh. Sara opened her eyes from her swoon to see Orpheo's mask-like expression half hid by the coils of the bullwhip. She looked around and saw Radh pumping violently into the small figure beneath him. The woman was pushing helplessly at his shoulders, and the sight of the near rape and domination filled Sara with anger. She brought the whip down onto the bobbing male buttocks, striking again and again to raise welts on the dark skin. The blows quickened the movements, and then suddenly the man grasped the woman's ass, their hips convulsing in unison. Sara dropped the whip with a cry and knelt between the four legs. Streaks of white male come were running out and covering the male shaft, and the sack behind the shaft quivered with its last discharges. Sara lowered her head, smelling the wonderful bitter smell of love consummated, then licked energetically at the residue, encouraging the last drops of balm into her own painful throat. They collapsed in a heap to the floor.

Sara awoke to the sight of Orpheo and the two other women clustered around a low wickerwork table. There were several implements on the table before them. Sara rose and looked them over. Several were small toothbrushlike items, except the bristles appeared to be tiny teeth. Several pots of dye, of brass patterned minutely with geometric designs, stood near the brushes. A tiny brass mallet and some medicinal-looking gauze and bottles completed the ensemble.

After a moment she knew what it was, and she hesitated. Going this way would brand her forever, would mark her publicly for what she was, and there was enough left of her white middle-class upbringing to raise unheard of objections. She saw Orpheo's gaze on her breast, and raised her hand protectively, then let it fall. The man waited patiently, no expression on his face. Vivian and Padmini, their eyes bright and their red lips open, were watching her with lust and fascination. They knew, without having been told, what their master wanted. They reached for Sara, grasping her soft pink breast firmly.

"No!" she cried.

Orpheo looked at her and smiled. Her heart melted. She would do this, he knew, by herself. Unforced by anything except her own conviction and desire.

He motioned the women away from Sara.

"But..." Padmini objected.

"You will have your chance. I know, you too want to enjoy this act. Wait. Sara will give her permission."

Instead, Sara knelt on the floor as gracefully as she could, reached for the wooden headrest, and placed it carefully under the back of her neck as she laid herself down.

Orpheo rose over her, one of the tattooing needles in his hand. It glinted blackly with the dye. Sara held her breasts up for him. He grasped one of the full mounds reverently.

At first it was a mere series of pinpricks, and she looked at him questioningly. Then he tapped lightly with the tiny mallet. Teeth bit into the aureole and Sara gave a gasp. Pleasure and pain, intermixed in tiny doses, lanced through her. She watched the process, her flesh jumping at each tap, her mind detached. She was conscious of a growing wetness in her cunt, a second rise of the powerful lusts that she had felt when Vivian was fucking her. When he finished, she was dizzy with the pain and lust. He kissed her breasts lightly, licking off the residue of bloody droplets. Her nipples, one stiff from the tattooing, rose even more at the soft loving touch.

"They would like to participate," Orpheo said gently, smiling into her tear-bedecked face. Sara nodded. Warm dark hands circled her other breast. Fingers explored her nipple, causing it to rise. The pressure increased, and Orpheo applied the needle again. The quivering of her flesh transmitted itself to the waiting, holding hands, and Sara knew that her sensations were being translated to her sisters.

Her hand stole to her cunt when it was over, and she massaged her clitoris. Her shoulders and rib cage were anchored to the grass mat with the strength of her determination, but her hips moved with abandon. Then her hand was pushed aside and a pair of gentle lips were applied to her hungry cunt, reinforcing and assuaging the waves of sensation that rippled from her tortured breast skin.

Sara's knees were brought up to her aching breasts. Another warm generous mouth lapped lovingly at her cunt, the broad knowledgeable tongue lapping the length of her lips, into the crevices and crannies only another woman would know. Once again she felt the tiny warning prick of the needles, and was lost in pleasure as the teeth bit in while the tongue continued its work.

A man rolled Sara gently over and parted her legs. She peered over her shoulder. Radh crouched there, then slid between her thighs head first. He began licking her clitoris and the length of her cunt. The touch was familiar and felt, in some indefinable way, like Padmini's. Yet it was unmistakably male mouth music that he was playing, demanding and fierce, coercing rather than teasing the pleasure out of her. She gave in to his demands, while the women applied themselves to her breasts and mouth. The first pinprick of the tattooing needles was almost a counterpoint, and her flesh shuddered again at the delicious mixture of pleasure and pain. She cried out at the first, incredibly sharp and pointed tap. But her hips stayed firmly on the demanding mouth, even as her mouth howled the pain and lust from each agonizing bite of the tattooing comb.

Chapter 14

"Where were you, the last few days on Tau'tevu?" Jo asked coquettishly. They were unpacking their suitcases in the flat they shared in Sydney, Sara deep in thought. "Summer romance, hey?"

Sara shrugged. "Something of the sort," she said briefly, her mind still on the events of the previous days. She was reluctant to leave, knowing she wanted to stay, and yet surrendering to the pull of her society and life. She knew she would carry the marks of her days on Tau'tevu with her wherever she went. Without thinking, she loosened the buttons on her blouse to allow more air to circulate against the skin that was beginning to glow in remembrance.

"What the hell is that?" Jo's voice brought her back from her reverie.

"What?" she spun around at the alarm on Jo's voice.

Her friend was looking at the dark mark that was half exposed on Sara's breast. "Oh no, Sara. Did you go and have one of these local tattoos put on? That's horrible! And these places are so unsanitary!"

Sara stood up proudly. She stared at Jo's incredulous eyes. "What the hell do *you* know?" She pulled open her blouse then dug in her print cotton bra. Jo watched, mesmerized. She had always envied Sara's large firm breasts, and, oddly, found she was uncomfortable looking at them. Sara pulled out her breast and held out the nipple for inspection. Jo drew in a startled breath. Around the pink-brown aureole was tattooed a dark circle composed of outward-facing smaller half circles, like a many-legged black spider crouched obscenely over the perfect pink mound.

"What...what is that?" Jo whispered breathlessly. The sight sent an unexplained shiver up her groin.

Sara smiled in inner triumph. "It's this," she explained, baring the second breast for a moment. Around the right nipple, faintly bruised blue on the surprisingly white flesh, Jo could see the marks of teeth, as if a mouth had closed forcefully, grinding perfect teeth into the flesh—the bite a lover might have made to stamp as an owner.

Sara looked at Jo, smiled again, then rose. "Do you want to know what it *means?*" She laughed gaily, and Jo again felt the shiver as the blue eyes held her own intently. "I don't think you'll understand."

Jo shook her head, and in sudden decision, Sara pulled at the waistband of her shorts and pulled her pants down.

It was not that Jo had not seen Sara's all before. When they had fucked the men on the beach, or in

TAU'TEVU

their room, she had inevitably seen all Sara had to offer. It had always affected her, made her uncomfortable, and she had always hidden the feeling from her roomie, and the reasons from herself. Now Sara allowed her, even encouraged her to look. The tanned rounded belly dipped into the valley between the golden thighs, then swelled slightly forward in white untanned skin where the bikini bottom had hidden the sun. Sara had a fine dark blonde bush, Jo saw approvingly, unconsciously touching her lips with the tip of her tongue. Then Sara turned, and Jo was startled from her contemplation of the swollen lips, hidden by the dark curly hair. The bikini mark covered half a buttock. On the white flesh, untouched by the sun, writhed a bluish black tattoo. Jo cried out in dismay at the desecration, while Sara looked over her shoulder in triumph.

She turned to face her roommate once again. Jo was looking at her in horrified attraction.

"Come here," Sara said in a commanding tone. She held her vulva cupped in her hand. Mesmerized Jo stepped closer. She expected a kiss, something to bridge the strangeness. Instead Sara grasped her by the nape and pushed her down using all her strength. Jo found herself on the floor on her knees, and Sara's full bush, smelling intimately and powerfully of a smell Jo had gotten used to in smaller doses from Sara's presence, covered her mouth. For an eternity the soft labial tissues rested on Jo's frozen mouth.

"Lick me!" it was less a whisper than a command. Hypnotized, Jo obeyed. Her tongue peeped nervously out, and for the first time she felt the taste of another woman. Sara's labia were soft and large, and she moved her hips so that Jo's hesitant tongue could touch every millimeter. Frozen by surprise, Jo did not know what to do except keep her tongue out and allow Sara to move as she willed. The firm hand on the back of her head kept her from moving.

"Lick me properly," Sara said again. This time her other hand slid down and parted her forest of hairs, then held open the outer lips, exposing the small hood and the tip of the clitoris. Jo closed her eyes and obeyed. The feel grew familiar with use, and at first Jo confined herself to licking the outside of the lips, then, with Sara's encouragement, she started putting her tongue deeply into Sara's interior. Sara was warm and moist, and a thrill of excitement ran through Jo's brain as she began to realize the power she had. She tired of licking, and started sucking the clitoral nubbin instead. One of her hands stole between her legs, hiking her short skirt and searching for her cunt, the other climbed up Sara's leg, feeling the muscular thigh, touching the full ass, then sliding between Sara's thighs to help keep the golden gate open. She was conscious of Sara's strong hand on her hair. She wanted to protest. The pulling was hurting her, and Sara was making it clear that she was being serviced by Jo, at Sara's pace, and for Sara's purposes. But the pleasure of doing what she was doing was too strong, and she feared that if she withdrew, or protested, Sara would withhold herself. And suddenly, Jo realized, that above all things in the world she wanted to please her roommate.

Sara's hand, which had been massaging her breasts in rhythm with Jo's licking, dropped to the dark-haired head beneath her. She started jerking her hips forward, forcing more of her mound onto Jo's face. Her nails dug into Jo's scalp.

"Suck me, Jo! Oh God, oh God, this is so good. Come on, you bitch. Stick that tongue in.... Ahaaaa."

Jo heard the words, but at first they were only sounds accompanying the sounds she made herself as she slurped noisily at Sara's hole. Then when they started making sense, she was too involved in the process of pleasing Sara, and found that she wanted to hear more. Because she *was* a bitch. A bitch in heat, and all she wanted was to please that golden fuzz that surrounded her mouth. So she licked and sucked away, and her own mumblings were padded by the rich flavor and softness of Sara's thighs.

"Oh Sara. You're so *sweet!* I'm so sorry we never did this before, honey. Oh wonderful. Let me...let me yes, more more." Her two hands were now gripping Sara's full buttocks and urging the blonde to even greater speeds as Sara ground her mound against Jo's willing face.

Sara quivered and gave a few harsh cries. "Fuck, fuck. Yes fuck you bitch. I'm going to give you the best...Suck me some more. Oh! Aaaaah." She quivered once again and her nails pulled at Jo's scalp as her vagina let down a flood of moisture.

She let go of Jo's head abruptly, and stepped back. Jo staggered forward, her elbows banging against the rug on the floor. She looked up in reproach. Sara was suddenly on her holding her down. Jo thought the position undignified, knees and elbows on the floor, her ass in the air. She had never let a man mount her that way, but Sara held her down in this position, whispering in her ear.

"Don't move. Wait! Let me!"

The whispering voice was full of promise, and Jo

stopped trying to rise, merely twisting her eyes around to see what Sara had in mind. The look on her roommate's face was startling, even scary. Only Sara's stroking hands, from Jo's nape, along her spine to the base between her buttocks, calmed Jo down. She licked her lips, exalting in the salty tastes of Sara's juices. Sara bent and licked her friend's back. Her tongue made circles and lines on the taut skin and Jo sighed in anticipation. One of Sara's hands was between her buttocks. At first, Sara could not find the correct entrance and Jo jerked when an exploring finger rubbed against her anal port, but soon Sara's soothing finger was parting Jo's wet lips and inserting itself into her expectant vagina.

Jo sighed, "Oh dear Sara. Oh dear, oh honey. I love that. I love that...."

Sara's hands and mouth became more demanding. She squeezed Jo's small breast, pinching the nipple lightly, while her other hand penetrated Jo with two fingers and her mouth rained kisses and small bites on Jo's back.

Jo shivered at the touch, small tremors running the length of her curled body. "Oh dear. Again, again, again. Please..."

"Do you like this? Do you want me to go on?" Sara was nibbling at her ear, and her warm breath almost drove Jo mad.

"Yes, please baby. Oh please.... I'd do anything for you, just please..."

"You like it that much?" There was a tinge of doubt in Sara's voice, and to emphasize her words she stuck another finger to the knuckle in Jo's cunt. "Would you do anything I said?"

"Yes, anything. Oh please Sara, please. Do it to me..." Jo was rocking forward and back, her voice so husky she herself could not recognize it.

"You *must* do anything I say," Sara teased. "Or I won't do this," she bit at Jo's nape, a nip that pinched an hurt. "Or this," and her hand squeezed Jo's breast firmly, while the other dug deeper into Jo's wetness.

"Anything, oh anything. Don't stop. I'm yours. I really am. Please Sara, please..."

Sara slid suddenly back, her hands parting Jo's buttocks. Jo instinctively raised her ass higher in the air. The touch of Sara's tongue sent electricity raging through her body. It was even better than she had expected, better than she had ever imagined. Sara drove her tongue deep into her waiting cunt hole, her hands pulling Jo's asscheeks apart almost viciously. Jo rocked back onto the probing tongue.

"Oh Sara! Oh Sara!" she was conscious that she was wailing now, her whole body simply demanding more of the probing firm wetness.

Sara shifted her position, and her tongue was now at the higher entrance, licking and probing. Jo tried to move away, uncomfortable, though desirous, at the intrusion into an area she had thought reserved for other things. A sharp double slap on her buttocks stopped her, and she began to realize that Sara's actions were not an unaimed or unconsidered probe. Bemused, Jo held herself tense, then gradually relaxed as Sara's tongue laved the exterior of her anus, then drove deeply into the reluctant muscle ring.

"Oh, Sara. Not there," she moaned, still not over her initial surprise. "Please, don't stop," she said in confusion, and Sara's tongue continued probing into her. She felt herself reach a climax as Sara started long strokes the length of Jo's crack. She trembled, her entire body convulsing as an eruption started in her groin and arose to her hindbrain.

"OOOaaaaaaaah" she was screaming, her nails digging into her own flesh, while Sara suddenly mounted her from behind. Sara's hips ground against her buttocks, her hands clutched at Jo's breasts, pulling and twisting the nipples. Her mouth descended, biting and nipping at Sara's sweat-beaded neck and shoulders, and she humped her hips like a man at Jo's willing body.

They slumped in exhaustion, the blonde clutching the brunette to her. Then Sara rose, and pulled Jo to her feet. She kissed her deeply, then laid her on the bed. Parting Jo's legs, she looked long and thoroughly at Jo's cunt. At first Jo was embarrassed, and she moved uneasily, but Sara stopped her movements with a slap.

She rose from the bed and looked down at her friend. "Did you really mean that? That you would do anything?"

Jo looked up at her, her eyes moistening. "How can you doubt that? After what we've done? Oh Sara dear, anything, anything you want…"

Sara smiled an enigmatic smile and turned to the chest of drawers on the other side of the room, where she had been unpacking.

Sara returned from the drawer. Her cunt hairs were moist, and to Jo, lying spread-eagle on the bed, she was the most desirable thing in the world. But Sara was carrying a long, black, snaky object in her hands. A braided leather whip. And she had a look in her eyes that made Jo shudder. She found that she was yearning for the whip. Her insides warmed up at the sight, and she realized that there was nothing more she wanted than to give herself to the pleasure of having Sara—Sara!—use the whip on her. Her belly quivered as Sara slowly drew the lash between her fingers, then passed it down, moistening it from the damp collection of their juices at the juncture of her thighs. The lash rubbed against Sara's clitoris, emerging shinier than it had been. Jo's eyes, mesmerized, followed its progress as Sara's hand rose.

"No!" she called out suddenly overcome by fear. Panting, she moved back, only to see Sara staring at her in triumph, something of a sneer in her face. Jo turned tail and ran from the room, ran from the flat, her clothes in her hand, into the welcoming night air.

Chapter 15

Jo had walked around and around the neighborhood for hours, stopping at a café to calm her nerves. But when she walked into the flat, Sara was gone. So were her suitcase and some clothes. It did not take Jo long to figure out where her friend had gone, and a simple call to their travel agent confirmed her suspicions. Sara had departed thirty minutes before on an available seat. Back to Tau'tevu. And the bullwhip had gone with her. Jo felt a flutter at the pit of her stomach when she recalled the scene, and the memory of Sara, striding over to her, the lash trailing from her fingers and between her legs sent unfamiliar, almost romantic feelings, welling up in her.

Jo's first reaction was to say "good riddance" to herself. But her own body denied her. And she knew she had to save her friend from whatever horrid fate awaited her on the island. She made another call, and found herself the following day, alone in a crowd of roistering, half-drunk tourists, on her way back to the island. Red rimmed eyes, full of determination, and a need to rescue her friend all bundled together, she checked into a hotel.

She found that she did not know where to start. Sara had probably arrived, but she had vanished from sight. Jo wandered through the *kanak* and Indian neighborhoods, through the tourist areas for two days, asking about a tall blonde tourist. She even mentioned the tattoo, and checked out several tattoo parlors, but besides countless personal propositions, many of which included tattooing her for free, if only in places hidden by her bikini, no one had done any of the designs she described.

In the evening of the second day, dispirited and alone, she sat nursing a beer at Kimball's. The tables were full of noisy, boisterous tourists, and she was constantly jostled by beer-smelling men, and some women, accidentally or on purpose. One table was quieter than the rest. Two men and two women sat there quietly, immobile, almost not talking. One of the men, the one with a European face, looked vaguely familiar. She thought she had seen him the last time she had been in the bar, almost way back in history, before she had started this lunatic quixotic quest. The women were also striking. One was a slim Indian woman, her long hair shining, her bright eyes glowing in a dark, finely boned face. The other was a large *kanak*, who would have looked overweight but for the obvious grace with which she carried herself. The fourth man was a copy of the Indian woman, obviously brother and sister.

They rose to go, passing near Jo's seat. A passer-by staggered into the Indian girl, and she put a hand on Jo's table to steady herself, then moved on, flashing a brilliant smile of apology at the bemused Jo. They had walked out of the bar before Jo realized that something on the girl's wrist had attracted her attention. Then it came to her. The girl wore a bracelet of curved shell pieces that emulated almost exactly the pattern tattooed on Sara's breast! Hurriedly, Jo rose and followed the foursome. They were far down the beach, but the moon was approaching its quarter, and Jo could see them walking along the sand. She hurried after them, her heart pounding. Perhaps the bracelet was a coincidence, but she had nothing better to go on.

The sand proved hard going, but the people in front of her kept ahead only by a margin. They walked down the beach, away from the tourist areas, past the fishing boats of the locals, drawn up on the beach for the night. The sounds and smells of the tropical night were all around her. Jo picked up her pace as the foursome passed through the inhabited areas to a dark point that stuck out into the sea. There were no habitations around, and the wind sighed strongly in the palm above her head. They vanished in the shade of some trees the moonlight could not penetrate. She speeded up, finding herself about thirty yards behind them. She was breathing hard, and yet her jaw dropped further. None of the four were now wearing any clothes, and their arms were about one another. She slowed, slowed some more as they turned from the beach through a fence of bamboo palings. A single house stood there, constructed in the native fashion of poles and woven grass, but larger than any she had seen before. She peered through the fence just in time to see the four figures vanish in the house.

Jo dithered. She did not know whether to knock on the door and inquire, or whether to simply forget the whole thing and get on the plane back home. As she stood there, she heard a sound that set her hair on end. From within the house, muffled by the walls, she heard a familiar voice cry out.

"Oh God! Yes! Oh God! Again, again."

It was Sara's voice. Creeping forward, Jo grew suddenly bold, straightened herself and marched up to the front door. As she got closer, she heard, interspersed with Sara's cries, the unpleasant swishing sound, followed by a smack, of someone being beaten.

Jo's outrage knew no bounds. She leapt up the stairs of the verandah before the house, and heeding only the need of her friend, she stormed inside. She followed the sound through a complex of rooms. The Indian woman she had seen earlier was on her knees, her hands tied behind her with glistening silken cords. Behind her stood Sara, stark naked. She held a horse whip of raffia in her hand. With each stroke against the dark girl's bottom, she yelled like a banshee.

"What?...what are you *doing?*" Jo's voice was quavering. "I've been looking all over for you!"

Sara did not stop in her beating stroke, and her face was turned toward the other woman, not Jo.

A man stepped into view. The handsome dark face was in profile to Jo. He ignored the interloper, merely stepping up to Sara and running his hands over her body, pinching her buttocks and tits. He had a long, thin, dark cock, and it jutted before him like a mast. He poked it at the kneeling girl, and she obligingly opened her mouth and sucked him totally in, her throat distended. When he pulled himself out, the cock seemed to trail, wet and glistening, almost forever.

"You too, Sara," another male voice said. Jo turned as if bitten by a snake. A man was reclining there on a couch. The man was handsome in a hawk-faced sort of fashion. His lazy eyes were watching the scene. It was the man from Kimball's.

"Join Padmini, Sara," he said again.

Sara fell to her knees and brought her face to the long shaft where it emerged from Padmini's lips. Her own lips and tongue started flicking at the lengthy morsel.

"Don't stop lashing Padmini!" he ordered, and Sara raised her left hand and obeyed. The raffia bundle slashed against the slighter girl's hidden crack.

Jo watched horrified. She wanted to stop this desecration, to pull Sara away from the depths she had fallen to. She took one step forward, then was arrested by more movement. From the same door from which the Indian man had stepped, another figure marched out. She was a dark, strongly built *kanak* woman whose full breasts swayed enticingly as she walked. She carried a flat, thin, flexible paddle, somewhat like the paddles the croupiers used, except that this one was delicately carved and painted in red and black. She watched the scene, completely at ease under Jo's appalled gaze.

"Vivian, help them," the man reclining on the broad couch said.

Vivian stepped forward, she knelt with her back to Jo. Her head joined the cluster near the man's penis, and Jo could only assume that she too was participating in mouthing his cock, something she herself did, but only reluctantly, with select lovers. Then Jo's palms grew moist, once her surprise had passed. The dark *kanak* girl raised the paddle and brought it down with a resounding slap on the man's taut ass cheeks. He gave a cry and thrust himself fully forward. Pulling back, he was forced forward again as a second slap sounded on his behind, which flushed a darker brown, almost black where the paddle hit. The two women, the pale and the dark one, started alternately smacking their willing victims. Besides the sounds of the instruments on flesh, the only sound was the man's cry, as he stood, his face turned blindly towards the ceiling, his hips jerking deeply into the bound woman's willing mouth.

The man on the couch turned his burning cool eyes to face Jo. "Join them!" he ordered.

Mesmerized, she took one step forward, then another. The man on the couch watched her, his eyes holding hers. She moved forward blindly, until she was stopped by the heat and the feel of the bodies in movement before her.

"Hold her!" the man on the couch said, and Jo was too late to turn as the other man grasped her elbows and pulled them high and back. Her eyes were still on Sara. Nonetheless, she managed to kick back at him, a move he had anticipated, and they moved forward in lock step.

The man on the couch rose. "I am Orpheo," he said in cultured tones. "The slim lady is Padmini, and holding you is Radh. The other is V'iaroaa'ave'ahine though we call her Vivian, and Sara you already know. Sara, would you please come here?"

Sara came to him, and without any warning, he

slashed her breasts hard with the flats of his palms. Mesmerized, Jo saw Sara's beautiful breasts jump and quiver, reddening where the palms had slapped against them. Sara's face grew softer, her lips moistened of their own accord, and Jo could not miss those signs of passion. She felt her own insides moisten in response, and then the movement of the man behind her brought her back down to earth.

The trance broke, and Jo struggled wildly in Radh's grip. He still held her tightly, his erect penis digging into the back of her cotton shorts.

"What the hell do you mean, treating us like this?" Jo's voice possessed all the acidity and outrage she was capable of.

Orpheo stared at her, his eyes blank. "I merely allow you to express your desires," he said, his voice perfectly even. "Nothing more."

"No! Never! Sara doesn't want this. *I* don't want this. You've just hypnotized, or drugged her, then, or something!! Let us *go!*" She was shouting, conscious that mixed with the outrage and the fear was something else, something she was frightened of more than she feared the people in the room. Orpheo nodded at Radh, and he bore her out of the room. Darkness closed about them, and blinded, struggling, she was eased out of her clothes then leashed by an unbreakable woven rattan collar and led to the solid hut frame. Time passed in darkness.

Light arrived after some indeterminate time in an ever increasing brightness. It allowed Jo to focus her eyes on the bare interior of the hut. And on Orpheo, his neck and limbs hung with primitive jewelry, his body naked, a massive erection announcing his intentions.

Shark's teeth, colored beads, woven feather and fur bands, and nuggets of raw gold and stones streaked with silver winked in the light. As did the tip of his immense penis, which had been painted in a delicate tracery of gold paint.

Jo crouched fearfully against the woven grass wall. She could feel her breasts press heavily against the tops of her thighs. The nipples were hard from the cold. The warrior stood before her, his tumescence jutting before him like a blunt lance. Her hands sweated and grains of dirt stuck to them. He moved a step forward and she could smell the lust on him. The slightly bitter smell from his crotch.

The dark knob, streaked with gold, was positioned above her forehead and she reared backwards her eyes looking up at him in panic. He swayed forward and the knob of his engorged cock was pressed at her lips. Without stopping to think or react she opened her lips and the knob pushed its way in. Fearfully she inhaled the spongy head like a child sucking a tit.

The tenseness in her body vanished. Her fears seemed to evaporate as she felt the unfamiliar, familiar sensation of a cock in her mouth. She had tried to be a good cocksucker ever since one of her boyfriends had told her roughly to improve her technique. But here, now, she realized that technique did not matter. That whatever failings she suffered, *he* would accept, or else he would repair and correct. In either case, it was not up to her, but to him alone. Exhilarated by the self-discovery, she pulled and sucked at the male pole, her energies no longer focused on possible criticism, but rather on the sheer pleasure she no longer noticed with others, of having an erect penis in her mouth. Eagerly, no longer fearfully, she set to work. When the pole started pulsing she no longer felt the urge to pull back, instead allowing the stream of bitter, salty, sticky fluid to fill her mouth. She rolled it on her tongue, swallowing some, letting the rest dribble down her chin without bothering to wipe it off.

The others entered the bare room. Her leash was uncoupled from the beam, and she was led to the large central room of the hut. An array of instruments lay on a small tabouret, and she eyed them fearfully but trustingly, knowing that they were for *her*, that they were inevitable, and thus less frightening. Then she remembered, her memory triggered by the sight of the whips, that she had come to search for Sara, and she looked around guiltily for her absent friend.

She had little time to look. She was pulled to the floor by the ring about her neck, and it was fastened to an elaborately carved stake. Crouched there, naked, her bottom high in the air, she watched without fear and with great interest as Orpheo selected a long flexible cane from the table, and raised it above his head. It came down on her buttocks with a long zipping sound, that ended with a flat crack that echoed the pain she felt in her buttocks. Her muscles tried to rise and run from the pain, but between her legs, her cunt spoke loudly, demanding more of the same, more of the expected but never before encountered sensation.

Orpheo beat her with long steady strokes. At first she merely quivered violently. Tears came to her eyes and she bit her lip. Then the moaning started, uncontrolled at first, she then saw how it affected her audience. Radh's long, thin black prick rose jerkily at each call that came from her mouth. Vivian had one hand on her own, and another on Padmini's breast. With each moan—with each of *her* moans—the strong square brown hand clenched on a soft mound. One of Padmini's hands was stuck fully into her own quim, exposing the long pink gash framed by black, and she too was crying out, staccato, almost formal yelps.

When she felt she would be unable to stand anymore, when her hips and thighs were at the end of their strength, the beating stopped. Orpheo knelt beside her, and raised her head as high as the leash allowed. His lips caressed her forehead, then fastened in a deep demanding kiss on her mouth. The lips she had bitten in her agony were swollen now, and terrifically sensitive. The laving of his tongue was a balm, which at the same time, aroused her hidden senses. Jo responded passionately, her own tongue dancing a counter-point to his.

He moved back and she lowered her head in submission once again. Another pair of legs stood behind her. Jo knew what to do this time, and she parted her knees further, exposing her cunt fully. Even that did not satisfy her, and she slipped her hand along her sweat-dampened belly, shuddering at the caress, until she could part the lips of her cunt, exposing the hole fully to the gaze of the entire company.

Padmini stood above her, her own eyes blazing. This petty servant, she thought, dared to interrupt a tryst with her prince. She raised the braided wire negligently, and brought it down slashing onto the pale buttocks before her. The silver flashed in the light, slapping into the quivering low-caste buttocks. Padmini smiled in creamy satisfaction as the slave-concubine jumped, as her mouth cried out. Padmini raised the lash again, angling her blow so that the strike would fall full on the ugly hairy cunt. The lower castes had no idea of hygiene, she knew, and they never prepared their mounds properly for their lovers. For a second she stroked her own glistening bare mound, and looked dreamily at her prince. He shook his head in denial, slightly, but that was enough for her. All contrite, she shifted her aim. *He* was not yet ready for the slave's final agony. Instead, with growing fervor, she brought the lash down again and again on the quivering buttocks and the shaking thighs, until the screams of the punished slave merged into one delicious, loud wail. And when she felt the blows raining down on her own backside, her happiness was complete.

The rain of blows against Jo's punished buttocks stung her like a scorpion she had once touched as a child. At first she tried to keep back her screams, but then she realized the futility and allowed her throat full rein. She was amazed to find, as her ass burned again and again at the vicious blows, that her fingers had found her clitoris and were massaging it with frantic demand. Her screaming took on a new timbre as she found herself trying to fulfill a demand she was unable to. Again and again she dipped into her cunt in concert with the wire that bit into her ass, hoping, praying, that someone would come to her aid, that someone would relieve her of the tremendous pressure that was building up in her cunt.

"Oh Lord! Please, please. Noooooo. Do it to me. Please someone fuck me! I neeeeed it!" came out as a continuous and unending wail, a demand of the flesh she could not refuse. The tenor of the blows changed, and she risked a look behind her. The Indian girl had stepped back, rubbing her ass with both hands. The other Indian, the man, now stood behind her and his hard palms were playing a drumming tattoo on her ass. And he had what she craved for most: a large erect prick rose from between his thighs, threatening her with its blind eye. So Jo did not resist when, with a show of unexpected strength, he flipped her over on her back. She spread her legs expectantly, reaching for the erect cock. It was warm and hard, and the fluid dripping from the hole, the transparent fluid of lust, not fulfillment, filled her palms with promise. He looked at her with blazing eyes as she manipulated her prick and tried to pull him on to her, and his hands reached for her body.

Radh's palms were stinging from the blows he had rained on Padmini's jiggling yet firm ass. His rage had built at her infidelity, and now this strange, short-haired white woman was trying to manipulate him as well. The bitch, he thought, and he started slapping her welcoming body. Her soft breasts jiggled at his touch and even through the slapping movement of his palms he could feel the erect tiny stiffness of her nipples. Enraged, he played with her body like a set of drums. His fingers flicked at her sensitive nipples, and rippled on her belly with resounding slaps. She screamed in counterpoint to his own mouthings, "Yes, oh yes. Please. Take me. Fuck me any way you want. Please, please, please!"

His hands descended to her obscenely hairy mound and he slapped her violently. Her own hand was there, not protecting her femininity, but opening it for him, exposing the pink interior. He slapped harder, and each movement brought her fingers deeper into her cunt. Unable to help himself, he lowered his head and mouthed at her flesh. His teeth sank into her white breasts, leaving red crescent marks. Then, as she tried to force his hands into her, he lowered his head rapidly between her thighs and bit at the fleshy excrescences of her cunt.

"Yes, more! That's it, you bastard! More, put your tongue in there!" Jo was almost hysterical with relief. He had finally divined her need, and his mouth and tongue were engaged with the core of her femininity. Completely out of control, her body dictating her actions, she started jerking her hips into the air, into the welcoming, hurtful, demanding mouth.

Another figure stood above her. It was Vivian, and in her hand she held the *muloko'ewa*. Her face set into hard lines, she raised the instrument and brought it down fully onto Jo's breasts. Jo screamed again, shuddered, tried to move away as the lash was raised again.

Vivian looked down at the captive. The woman below her should not move, and she placed one of her feet squarely on the other's face to keep her in place. Once again she raised the instrument of chiefly punishment, knowing that she herself was now a chief, speaking for *her* chief, and so on, back into the dimness of history and the island. She raised the *muloko'ewa* again and brought it down in a slashing motion against the pale mounds beneath her. As she struck, she gradually sank down, the period between her blows quickened until a rain of unending blows hit the captive. And still the captive squealed, through the masking foot. V'iaroaa'ave'ahine knew what to do. She removed her foot from the squealing mouth, and straddled the captive's head, bringing her own weight to bear in a vicious downward jerk.

Jo felt herself choking, and she took a great breath of air as soon as the hard foot was removed from her face. She was whimpering with the mixture of pain and passion, but mostly from the frustration of desire that coursed through her veins, to which the bites on her cunt and the blows on her breast were merely fuel. She knew it was the end when the damp, earthy-smelling cunt descended to cover her face. She strove at first to remove the weight, then she realized that this was what she had come for, and her body fell back. She floated in a sea of pleasure and pain, real sensations she had never felt before under the thin veneer of her upbringing, and though her body still screamed for more, she was content.

All sensation was suddenly removed from her body with an abruptness that left her gasping like a fish out of water. She opened her eyes. The others stood away from her, in a small group. The absence of sensations she now knew she craved was shattering. Automatically she rose to her feet. She knew she should walk out. Something terrible was happening to her, she knew that. After all, wasn't the occasional grope in a car, the odd bloke she found at a pub, the chance of marriage and regular hoggings what sex was about? She took one step to the door, then saw the four others looking at her, their faces immobile.

"Please," she cried, falling to her knees. "Please let me."

The four watched her impassively. She crawled toward them still muttering, "Please, please." Nearing them, almost smelling the skin, she knew suddenly what she had to do. She fell flat on her belly, her body full length on the polished wooden floor. Inching forward like that, her head touched someone. Blindly she raised her head and began kissing the foot. She spread herself on the floor, surrounded by a forest of legs. She blindly turned her head and reached for the nearest foot. Her lips closed around the willing member. She moved from one to another, always imploring, knowing, somehow, that *this* was the way she had really wanted it. Knowing also that she had to go through with it all to find herself.

Orpheo stepped back and seated himself once again on the broad couch, which had been laid with rich Indian fabrics that almost hurt Jo's eyes with their explosion of color.

"Sara!" he said in a low voice, and Jo realized, in a blinding flash, that this was what she had been waiting for.

The hanging across one of the doorways was brushed aside and Jo saw Sara standing there. It was a Sara she had never seen before. Her friend was naked. Her upper arms and thighs were decorated with shell and teeth bands that dug into her flesh. Her black tattoos had been rubbed with oil and they shone darkly in the light. Her blonde hair was pulled high above her head, giving her normally rather rotund face a severity Jo had only seen on the night of their quarrel. She carried a leather stockman's whip of braided leather, and wore knee high brown riding boots.

"Sara!" Jo said, her voice beseeching. She licked her lips. This was not the way. With what dignity she could muster, she turned her back to Sara. Her hands went behind her own body, and she grasped the mounds of her buttocks and pulled, exposing the length of the crack, the tiny button of her anus, the full lips of her cunt. Awkwardly, yet with a strange grace she sank to the carpeted floor.

"Please beat me, Sara," she said in a firm voice. "Please have me." She looked back, her eyes full on her friend. Sara's face was impassive, but her eyes were full of tears, and there was a flush of happiness on her skin. Slowly, almost dreamily, she raised her hand.

"Only three," she said.

"As many as you want," Jo said.

The first blow was crosswise to her thighs. Jo fell forward onto her elbows, her breasts mashed against the carpet, bruised nipples leaping to life with a tingle that sent a shudder through Jo's upper torso. But these sensations were nothing more than a sideshow, for Jo's entire frame was trembling from the ferocity of the pain that rode up her from the touch of the whip on her thighs. She cried out in full throat, knowing that there was no point in hiding the pain, yet delighting in the sensation.

"Oh, oahh. Oh, oh," she gasped as she pulled herself back again. Her flesh shrank at the movement, knowing what was to come. The second blow was worse than the first, cutting deeply into her marked buttocks, magnifying the pain from the first lash. Now, she knew, would come the real tests, and she braced herself for it, parting her buttocks against the pain, molding her own shuddering flesh to the indomitable will of her lust. Sara raised the whip, hesitated for a second, then when she saw the determination on her friend's face, she brought the lash down in a vertical blow that struck Jo the full length of her crack. It ended with a splat against the top of Jo's mound.

All breath was drawn out of Jo's lungs with the power of the pain. For a long minute she could not move, could not work her lungs. Then a shriek, of pain and of triumph, burst out of her as she collapsed on the floor. Darkness threatened to claim her, but suddenly she felt other hands parting her buttocks, and the soothing touch of Sara's tongue and lips on her tortured cunt. She felt Sara lick away the blood and the pain, soothe her flesh, and at the same time raise her sexuality to a fever pitch. There was no holding back now. Her insides convulsed and she shuddered, caught in the throes of an undeniable and unstoppable climax. A hot point at the pit of her belly erupted with spasms of pleasure so intense she felt as if she could not bear it. And the waves of pleasure went on and on, as Sara's demanding tongue sucked the last of her pleasure through her lips.

Sara moved aside, and a male member filled Jo's bruised cunt. He shafted into her, undeniably male, and Jo opened her eyes in time to see Orpheo's cruel mouth, now bent in a smile of almost gentle pleasure, descend onto her own. She met his thrusts with thrusts of her own hips, ignoring the superficial pain of the lacerations, actually glorying in them, and entwining her arms around the muscular shoulders. He exploded into her, spraying her with his male essence, and she sighed deeply, arcing her body in return, as she felt an orgasm to match his. Her insides, moistened by her own juices, were now flooded by the mixture, and she delighted in the squelching feeling between her legs as they moved.

The man rose from her and Jo could feel the wetness drool from the slit between her legs. A second heavy masculine body replaced the first, and she felt the blunt head of another cock fumbling at her gooey entrance. He moved into her, shifting the angle of his hips and thrusts, making sure every part of her vagina was touched, and she responded again with a climax that locked them together in deep embrace.

Jo raised her head. The lust was fully on her and she could only dig her fingers deeper into her own cunt to seek for relief. Fingers and palm were coated by the residue the men had left and she thrummed her prominent clitoris mercilessly with her hand, moaning in frustration. The light went on suddenly, and she was surrounded by her tormentors. She looked up and screamed. They were all naked but for identical shark-teeth necklaces and faces that had been painted in swirls and dots of a black matte color. Five erect cocks faced her, and the artificial ones worn by the women were even more threatening than the other two, for she knew she could expect no mercy from them.

A hand grabbed her hair and a warm male cock, still smelling of her own inner juices and the bitterness of male come, was thrust deeply into her mouth. She gagged, but essayed to lick as much of the male member as she could. It was withdrawn and the other replaced it. Again, exercising all her control she refrained from gagging and set to work to clean it from the results of its previous penetration of her insides.

One of the women lay on the rush-covered floor on her back. A long gold phallus stuck in the air at the juncture of her legs. Jo neither knew nor cared who it was. She was on her knees in a moment, crouched over the erect shaft, ramming herself deeply onto it, feeling relief flooding her interior along with the penetration.

Hands held her immobile, and she protested wordlessly, wanting to move, to feel the incredible shaft ravaging her insides. The moan turned to a prolonged shriek as the *muloko'ewa* bit into her backside. Fire ravaged her ass and she contracted her muscles to get away, forcing herself deeper onto the golden shaft. More lashing followed until her ass was a mass of agony, burning fiercely. She wanted to escape the pain and humiliation, but knew she could not do this, could not abandon her own resolve.

Then she screamed again. One of the women, her large breasts banging against Jo's back, was bending over her. Without any preparation or lubrication save the sweat that had risen from the beating, the massive shaft the woman wore was positioned at the entrance of Jo's ass and driven in. She screamed again, high and loud as she felt the knob pass the restraining ring of muscle. Her rectum was on fire as she struggled to extricate herself. Hands grasped the three entwined figures and she was rolled over onto her back. The combined weights of herself and the slimmer woman who was fucking her cunt forced the rear shaft deeper into her ass. She whimpered as she felt the wiry cuntal hairs rub like sandpaper against her newly beaten buttocks, as the artificial cock tore into her ass.

Notwithstanding the agony she felt a pleasure rise as the two cocks inserted into her rubbed against one another inside her. Her moans of pain were turning into grunts of pleasure as both women, above and below her, started arching their hips and driving their shafts deeper into Jo's hungry orifices.

One of the men strode forward. He knelt between Jo's spread legs, behind the woman who was fucking her cunt. Breasts mashed into her own as the man added his weight. His fingers fumbled at the joint of Jo's cunt and the dildo that was working away at her. The man thrust forward, his cock joining the other. Jo screamed again, unable to contain the pain of the triple intrusion. Her ass was distended as far as it could go, and now she had two cocks in her cunt as well. Again and again she screamed as pain and lust intermingled and the three bodies pumped at her unmercifully. She was alone in the world with only savages ravaging her insides. Her hands made aimless motions, trying to keep them off, but her arms were seized and imprisoned by the second man who stood over the group. His cock was thrust unceremoniously into Jo's mouth, obscuring the actions of the other. The broad shaft filled her mouth, and she puffed her cheeks then hollowed them to accommodate it. Without attempting to consider her in any way, the man started pumping his cock into her mouth, muffling her cries.

He pulled back a second, not to give her rest but for the pleasure of letting her see Sara stride forth. Jo recognized her friend by the tattoos she had recently found so horrifying. Sara was carrying the stockman's whip, which she ran through her fingers and between her lips. The rest of her face was obscured by savage swirls of black paint. She raised the whip and brought it down onto Jo's exposed breast, held fast by the man pumping into her cunt. The man whose cock was in her mouth thrust forward just as she attempted to scream. A line of glowing fire reached from her breast through her spine to the very center of her being where three cocks pumped their might into her soft lacerated interior. She was ready for the unexpected pleasure as the second stroke fired her exposed thighs, and the third landed onto her exposed shoulders. This time, as she cried out onto the ravaging cock, it was a cry of surrender, triumph, and pleasure.

When it was over, before she slid into sleep on a silk-covered bed to which she had been carried, she felt her body. The bruised cunt and torn asshole hurt, and she was covered by sweat and the drying exudations of her lovers' remains. She knew that they could now do anything with her, and she was content. She fingered the silver-and-shark tooth torque she now wore around her neck. It could not be opened, and she knew she would wear it for the rest of her life. With sure fingers she forced the tips of the teeth deeper into her skin. Above her, Orpheo smiled his mysterious smile.

You've heard of the writers
but didn't know where to find them

Samuel R. Delany • Pat Califia • Carol Queen • Lars Eighner • Felice Picano • Lucy Taylor • Aaron Travis • Michael Lassell • Red Jordan Arobateau • Michael Bronski • Tom Roche • Maxim Jakubowski • Michael Perkins • Camille Paglia • John Preston • Laura Antoniou • Alice Joanou • Cecilia Tan • Michael Perkins • Tuppy Owens • Trish Thomas • Lily Burana

You've seen the sexy images
but didn't know where to find them

Robert Chouraqui • Charles Gatewood • Richard Kern • Eric Kroll • Vivienne Maricevic • Housk Randall • Barbara Nitke • Trevor Watson • Mark Avers • Laura Graff • Michele Serchuk • Laurie Leber

You can find them all in
Masquerade

a publication designed expressly for the connoisseur of the erotic arts.

ORDER TODAY
SAVE 50%
1 year (6 issues) for $15; 2 years (12 issues) for only $25!

Essential. —*Skin Two*

The best newsletter I have ever seen! —*Secret International*

Very informative and enticing. —*Redemption*

A professional, insider's look at the world of erotica. —*Screw*

I recommend a subscription to **MASQUERADE**... It's good stuff. —*Black Sheets*

MASQUERADE presents some of the best articles on erotica, fetishes, sex clubs, the politics of porn and every conceivable issue of sex and sexuality. —*Factsheet Five*

Fabulous. —*Tuppy Owens*

MASQUERADE is absolutely lovely ... marvelous images. —*Le Boudoir Noir*

Highly recommended. —*Eidos*

DIRECT

Masquerade/Direct • DEPT X74L • 801 Second Avenue • New York, NY 10017 • FAX: 212.986.7355
MC/VISA orders can be placed by calling our toll-free number: 800.375.2356

☐ PLEASE SEND ME A 1 YEAR SUBSCRIPTION FOR ~~$30~~ *NOW* $15!
☐ PLEASE SEND ME A 2 YEAR SUBSCRIPTION FOR ~~$60~~ *NOW* $25!

NAME _____
ADDRESS _____
CITY _____ STATE _____ ZIP _____
TEL ( ) _____
PAYMENT: ☐ CHECK ☐ MONEY ORDER ☐ VISA ☐ MC
CARD # _____ EXP. DATE _____

ROSEBUD BOOKS

THE ROSEBUD READER
Rosebud has contributed greatly to the burgeoning genre of lesbian erotica—to the point that authors like Lindsay Welsh, Aarona Griffin and Valentina Cilescu are among the hottest and most closely watched names in lesbian and gay publishing. Here are the finest moments from **Rosebud**'s contemporary classics. $5.95/319-8

K. T. BUTLER

TOOLS OF THE TRADE
A sparkling mix of lesbian erotica and humor. An encounter with ice cream, cappuccino and chocolate cake; an affair with a complete stranger; a pair of faulty handcuffs; and love on a drafting table. Seventeen delightful tales. $5.95/420-8

LOVECHILD

GAG
From New York's thriving poetry scene comes this explosive volume of work from one of the bravest, most cutting young writers you'll ever encounter. The poems in *Gag* take on American hypocrisy with uncommon energy, and announce Lovechild as a writer of unique and unforgettable rage. $5.95/369-4

ALISON TYLER

BLUE SKY SIDEWAYS & OTHER STORIES
A collection of stories from the mastermind behind the sexy shenanigans of *Dial "L" for Loveless*. Here Tyler turns her eye toward a variety of women, and their many breathtaking experiences with lovers, friends—and even the occasional sexy stranger. From blossoming young beauties to fearless vixens, Tyler's stories find the sexy pleasures of everyday life. $6.50/394-5

DIAL "L" FOR LOVELESS
Meet Katrina Loveless—a private eye talented enough to give Sam Spade a run for his money. In her first solo case, Katrina investigates a murder implicating a host of society's darlings—including Tessa and Baxter Saint Claire (heirs to an unimaginable fortune), and the lovely, tantalizing, infamous Geneva twins. Loveless is just the investigator to untangle the ugly mess—even while working herself into a variety of highly compromising knots with the many lovelies who cross her path! $5.95/386-4

THE VIRGIN
Does he satisfy you? Is something missing? Maybe you don't need a man at all—maybe you need me. Veronica answers a personal ad in the "Women Seeking Women" category—and discovers a whole sensual world she never knew existed! And she never dreamed she'd be prized as a virgin all over again, by someone who would deflower her with a passion no man could ever show.... $5.95/379-1

THE BLUE ROSE
The tale of a modern sorority—fashioned after a Victorian girls' school. Ignited to the heights of passion by erotic tales of the Victorian age, a group of lusty young women are encouraged to act out their forbidden fantasies—all under the tutelage of Mistresses Emily and Justine, two avid practitioners of hard-core discipline! $5.95/335-X

ELIZABETH OLIVER

THE SM MURDER: Murder at Roman Hill
Intrepid lesbian P.I.s Leslie Patrick and Robin Penny take on a really hot case: the murder of the notorious Felicia Roman. The circumstances of the crime lead the pair on an excursion through the leatherdyke underground, where motives—and desires—run deep. But as Leslie and Robin soon find, every woman harbors her own closely guarded secret.... $5.95/353-8

ROSEBUD BOOKS

PAGAN DREAMS
Cassidy and Samantha plan a vacation at a secluded bed-and-breakfast, hoping for a little personal time alone. Their hostess, however, has different plans. The lovers are plunged into a world of dungeons and pagan rites, as the merciless Anastasia steals Samantha for her own. B&B—B&D-style!
$5.95/295-7

SUSAN ANDERS

CITY OF WOMEN
A collection of stories dedicated to women and the passions that draw them together. Designed strictly for the sensual pleasure of women, Anders' tales are set to ignite flames of passion from coast to coast. The residents of *City of Women* hold the key to even the most forbidden fantasies. $5.95/375-9

PINK CHAMPAGNE
Tasty, torrid tales of butch/femme couplings—from a writer more than capable of describing the special fire ignited when opposites collide. Tough as nails or soft as silk, these women seek out their antitheses, intent on working out the details of their own personal theory of difference. $5.95/282-5

LAVENDER ROSE

Anonymous

A classic collection of lesbian literature. From the writings of Sappho, Queen of the island Lesbos, to the turn-of-the-century *Black Book of Lesbianism*; from *Tips to Maidens* to *Crimson Hairs*, a recent lesbian saga—here are the great but little-known lesbian writings and revelations. A one volume survey of hot lesbian writing. $4.95/208-6

LAURA ANTONIOU, EDITOR

LEATHERWOMEN II
A follow-up volume to the popular and controversial *Leatherwomen*. Laura Antoniou turns an editor's discerning eye to the writings of women on the edge—resulting in a collection sure to ignite libidinal flames. Leave taboos behind, because these Leatherwomen know no limits.... $4.95/229-9

LEATHERWOMEN
These fantasies, from the pens of new or emerging authors, break every rule imposed on women's fantasies. The hottest stories from some of today's newest and most outrageous writers make this an unforgettable exploration of the female libido. $4.95/3095-4

AARONA GRIFFIN

PASSAGE AND OTHER STORIES
An S/M romance. Lovely Nina is frightened by her lesbian passions, until she finds herself infatuated with a woman she spots at a local café. One night Nina follows her, and finds herself enmeshed in an endless maze leading to a world where women test the edges of sexuality and power. A wildly popular title. $4.95/3057-1

VALENTINA CILESCU

MISTRESS WITH A MAID I: MY LADY'S PLEASURE
Dr. Claudia Dungarrow, a lovely, powerful, but mysterious figure at St. Matilda's College, comes face to face with desires that might prove the undoing of an ordinary woman. For when her hungers lead her to attempt seducing the virginal Elizabeth Stanbridge, she sets off a chain of events that eventually ruins her career. But Claudia vows revenge—and has it in her power to make her foes pay deliciously.... $5.95/412-7

ROSEBUD BOOKS

THE ROSEBUD SUTRA
"Women are hardly ever known in their true light, though they may love others, or become indifferent towards them, may give them delight, or abandon them, or may extract from them all the wealth that they possess." So says *The Rosebud Sutra*—a volume promising women's inner secrets. One woman learns to use these secrets in a quest for pleasure with a succession of lady loves.... $4.95/242-6

THE HAVEN
J craves domination, and her perverse appetites lead her to the Haven: the isolated sanctuary Ros and Annie call home. Soon J forces her way into the couple's world, bringing unspeakable lust and cruelty into their lives. $4.95/165-9

MISTRESS MINE
Sophia Cranleigh sits in prison, accused of authoring the "obscene" *Mistress Mine*. For Sophia has led no ordinary life, but has slaved and suffered—deliciously—under the hand of the notorious Mistress Malin. How long had she languished under the dominance of this incredible beauty? $5.95/445-3

LINDSAY WELSH

NASTY PERSUASIONS
A hot peek into the behind-the-scenes operations of Rough Trade—one of the world's most famous lesbian clubs. Join Slash, Ramone, Cherry and many others as they bring one another to the height of torturous ecstasy—all in the name of keeping Rough Trade the premier name in sexy entertainment for women. $6.50/436-4

MILITARY SECRETS
Colonel Candice Sproule heads a highly specialized boot camp. Assisted by three dominatrix sergeants, Col. Sproule takes on the talented submissives sent to her by secret military contacts. Then comes Jesse Robbins—whose pleasure in being served matches the Colonel's own. This new recruit sets off fireworks in the barracks—and beyond.... $5.95/397-X

ROMANTIC ENCOUNTERS
Beautiful Julie, the most powerful editor of romance novels in the industry, spends her days igniting women's passions through books—and her nights fulfilling those needs with a variety of lovers. Finally, through a sizzling series of coincidences, Julie's two worlds come together explosively! $5.95/359-7

THE BEST OF LINDSAY WELSH
A collection of this popular writer's best work. This author was one of Rosebud's early bestsellers, and remains highly popular. A sampler set to introduce some of the hottest lesbian erotica to a wider audience. $5.95/368-6

NECESSARY EVIL
What's a girl to do? When her Mistress proves too systematic, too by-the-book, one lovely submissive takes the ultimate chance—choosing and creating a Mistress who'll fulfill her heart's desire. Little did she know how difficult it would be—and, in the end, rewarding.... $5.95/277-9

A VICTORIAN ROMANCE
Lust-letters from the road. A young Englishwoman realizes her dream—a trip abroad under the guidance of her eccentric maiden aunt. Soon, the young but blossoming Elaine comes to discover her own sexual talents, as a hot-blooded Parisian named Madelaine takes her Sapphic education in hand. $5.95/365-1

A CIRCLE OF FRIENDS
The author of the nationally best-selling *Provincetown Summer* returns with the story of a remarkable group of women. Slowly, the women pair off to explore all the possibilities of lesbian passion, until finally it seems that there is nothing—and no one—they have not dabbled in. $4.95/250-7

ROSEBUD BOOKS

PRIVATE LESSONS
A high voltage tale of life at The Whitfield Academy for Young Women—where cruel headmistress Devon Whitfield presides over the in-depth education of only the most talented and delicious of maidens. Elizabeth Dunn arrives at the Academy, where it becomes clear that she has much to learn—to the delight of Devon Whitfield and her randy staff of Mistresses! $4.95/116-0

BAD HABITS
What does one do with a poorly trained slave? Break her of her bad habits, of course! The story of the ultimate finishing school, *Bad Habits* was an immediate favorite with women nationwide. "Talk about passing the wet test!... If you like hot, lesbian erotica, run—don't walk—and pick up a copy of *Bad Habits*."—*Lambda Book Report* $5.95/446-1

ANNABELLE BARKER

MOROCCO
A luscious young woman stands to inherit a fortune—if she can only withstand the ministrations of her cruel guardian until her twentieth birthday. With two months left, Lila makes a bold bid for freedom, only to find that liberty has its own excruciating and delicious price.... $4.95/148-9

A.L. REINE

DISTANT LOVE & OTHER STORIES
In the title story, Leah Michaels and her lover, Ranelle, have had four years of blissful, smoldering passion together. When Ranelle is out of town, Leah records an audio "Valentine:" a cassette filled with erotic reminiscences.... $4.95/3056-3

RHINOCEROS BOOKS

GERI NETTICK WITH BETH ELLIOT

MIRRORS: PORTRAIT OF A LESBIAN TRANSSEXUAL
The alternately heartbreaking and empowering story of one woman's long road to full selfhood. Born a male, Geri Nettick knew something just didn't fit. And even after coming to terms with her own gender dysphoria—and taking steps to correct it—she still fought to be accepted by the lesbian feminist community to which she felt she belonged. A fascinating, true tale of struggle and discovery. $6.95/435-6

TRISTAN TAORMINO & DAVID AARON CLARK, EDITORS

RITUAL SEX
While many people believe the body and soul to occupy almost completely independent realms, the many contributors to *Ritual Sex* know—and demonstrate—that the two share more common ground than society feels comfortable acknowledging. From personal memoirs of ecstatic revelation, to fictional quests to reconcile sex and spirit, *Ritual Sex* delves into forbidden areas with gusto, providing an unprecedented look at private life. $6.95/391-0

TAMMY JO ECKHART

PUNISHMENT FOR THE CRIME
Five scalding tales of power, pleasure and pain from an uncompromising writer. Peopled by characters of rare depth, the stories in *Punishment for the Crime* explore the true meaning of dominance and submission, and offer some surprising revelations. From an encounter between two of society's most despised individuals, to the explorations of longtime friends, these tales take you where few others have ever dared.... $6.95/427-5

RHINOCEROS BOOKS

THOMAS S. ROCHE, EDITOR

NOIROTICA: An Anthology of Erotic Crime Stories

A collection of darkly sexy tales, taking place at the crossroads of the crime and erotic genres. Thomas S. Roche has gathered together some of today's finest writers of sexual fiction, all of whom explore the murky terrain where desire runs irrevocably afoul of the law. $6.95/390-2

DAVID MELTZER

UNDER

Under is the story of a sex professional whose life at the bottom of the social heap is, nevertheless, filled with incident. Other than numerous surgeries designed to increase his physical allure, he is faced with an establishment intent on using any body for genetic experiments. These forces drive the cyber-gigolo underground—where even more bizarre cultures await.... $6.95/290-6

ORF

He is the ultimate musician-hero—the idol of thousands, the fevered dream of many more. And like many musicians before him, he is misunderstood, misused—and totally out of control. Every last drop of feeling is squeezed from a modern-day troubadour and his lady love. $6.95/110-1

AMARANTHA KNIGHT, EDITOR

SEX MACABRE

A new volume of horror tales designed for dark and sexy nights. Amarantha Knight—the woman behind the Darker Passions series, as well as the spine-tingling anthologies *Flesh Fantastic* and *Love Bites*—has gathered together erotic stories sure to make your skin crawl, and heart beat faster. $6.95/392-9

FLESH FANTASTIC

Humans have long toyed with the idea of "playing God": creating life from nothingness, bringing life to the inanimate. Now Amarantha Knight, author of the "Darker Passions" series of erotic horror novels, collects stories exploring not only the allure of Creation, but the lust that follows.... $6.95/352-X

RENE MAIZEROY

FLESHLY ATTRACTIONS

Lucien Hardanges was the son of the wantonly beautiful actress, Marie-Rose Hardanges. When she decides to let a "friend" introduce her son to the pleasures of love, Marie-Rose could not have foretold the erotic excesses that would lead to her own ruin and that of her cherished son. $6.95/299-X

LAURA ANTONIOU, EDITOR

NO OTHER TRIBUTE

A collection of stories sure to challenge Political Correctness in a way few have before, with tales of women kept in bondage to their lovers by their deepest passions. Love pushes these women beyond acceptable limits, rendering them helpless to deny the men and women they adore. $6.95/294-9

SOME WOMEN

Over forty essays written by women actively involved in consensual dominance and submission. Professional mistresses, lifestyle leatherdykes, whipmakers, titleholders—women from every conceivable walk of life lay bare their true feelings about explosive issues. $6.95/300-7

BY HER SUBDUED

These tales all involve women in control—of their lives, their loves, their men. So much in control that they can remorselessly break rules to become powerful goddesses of the men who sacrifice all to worship at their feet. $6.95/281-7

RHINOCEROS BOOKS

JEAN STINE
THRILL CITY
Thrill City is the seat of the world's increasing depravity, and Jean Stine's classic novel transports you there with a vivid style you'd be hard pressed to ignore. No writer is better suited to describe the unspeakable extremes of this modern Babylon. $6.95/411-9

SEASON OF THE WITCH
"A future in which it is technically possible to transfer the total mind...of a rapist killer into the brain dead but physically living body of his female victim. Remarkable for intense psychological technique. There is eroticism but it is necessary to mark the differences between the sexes and the subtle altering of a man into a woman." —*The Science Fiction Critic* $6.95/268-X

JOHN WARREN
THE TORQUEMADA KILLER
Detective Eva Hernandez has finally gotten her first "big case": a string of vicious murders taking place within New York's SM community. Piece by piece, Eva assembles the evidence, revealing a picture of a world misunderstood and under attack—and gradually comes to understand her own place within it. A hot, edge-of-the-seat thriller. $6.95/367-8

THE LOVING DOMINANT
Everything you need to know about an infamous sexual variation—and an unspoken type of love. Mentor—a longtime player in the dominance/submission scene—guides readers through this world and reveals the too-often hidden basis of the D/S relationship: care, trust and love. $6.95/218-3

GARY BOWEN
DIARY OF A VAMPIRE
"Gifted with a darkly sensual vision and a fresh voice, [Bowen] is a writer to watch out for." —Cecilia Tan

The chilling, arousing, and ultimately moving memoirs of an undead—but all too human—soul. Bowen's Rafael, a red-blooded male with an insatiable hunger for the same, is the perfect antidote to the effete malcontents haunting bookstores today. *Diary of a Vampire* marks the emergence of a bold and brilliant vision, firmly rooted in past *and* present. $6.95/331-7

GRANT ANTREWS
SUBMISSIONS
Once again, Antrews portrays the very special elements of the dominant/submissive relationship with restraint—this time with the story of a lonely man, a winning lottery ticket, and a demanding dominatrix. $6.95/207-8

MY DARLING DOMINATRIX
When a man and a woman fall in love, it's supposed to be simple, uncomplicated, easy—unless that woman happens to be a dominatrix. Curiosity gives way to unblushing desire in this story of one man's awakening to the joys to be experienced as the willing slave of a powerful woman. $6.95/447-X

LAURA ANTONIOU WRITING AS "SARA ADAMSON"
THE TRAINER
The Marketplace Trilogy comes to its thrilling close! The ultimate underground sexual realm includes not only willing slaves, but the exquisite trainers who take submissives firmly in hand. And now these mentors divulge the desires that led them to become the ultimate figures of authority. $6.95/249-3

RHINOCEROS BOOKS

THE SLAVE
This second volume in the "Marketplace" trilogy further elaborates the world of slaves and masters. *The Slave* covers the experience of one talented submissive who longs to join the ranks of those who have proven themselves worthy of entry into the Marketplace. But the price, while delicious, is staggeringly high....
$6.95/173-X

THE MARKETPLACE
The nationally best-selling novel that kicked off the increasingly popular Marketplace Trilogy. "Merchandise does not come easily to the Marketplace.... They haunt the clubs and the organizations.... Some are so ripe that they intimidate the poseurs, the weekend sadists and the furtive dilettantes who are so endemic to that world. And they never stop asking where we may be found...."
$6.95/3096-2

DAVID AARON CLARK

SISTER RADIANCE
A chronicle of a most desperate obsession—rife with Clark's trademark vivisections of contemporary desires, sacred and profane. The vicissitudes of lust and romance are examined against a backdrop of urban decay and shallow fashionability in this testament to the allure—and inevitability—of the forbidden.
$6.95/215-9

THE WET FOREVER
The story of Janus and Madchen—a small-time hood and a beautiful sex worker on the run from one of the most dangerous men they have ever known—*The Wet Forever* examines themes of loyalty, sacrifice, redemption and obsession amidst Manhattan's sex parlors and underground S/M clubs. Its combination of sex and suspense led Terence Sellers to proclaim it "evocative and poetic."
$6.95/117-9

ALICE JOANOU

BLACK TONGUE
"Joanou has created a series of sumptuous, brooding, dark visions of sexual obsession, and is undoubtedly a name to look out for in the future."
—*Redeemer*

Another seductive book of dreams from the author of the acclaimed *Tourniquet*. Exploring lust at its most florid and unsparing, *Black Tongue* is a trove of baroque fantasies—each redolent of forbidden passions. Joanou creates some of erotica's most mesmerizing and unforgettable characters.
$6.95/258-2

TOURNIQUET
A heady collection of stories and effusions from the pen of one our most dazzling young writers. Strange tales abound, from the story of the mysterious and cruel Cybele, to an encounter with the sadistic entertainment of a bizarre after-hours cafe. These strange, sexy tales are a sumptuous feast for all the senses.
$6.95/3060-1

CANNIBAL FLOWER
The provocative debut volume from this acclaimed writer.
"She is waiting in her darkened bedroom, as she has waited throughout history, to seduce the men who are foolish enough to be blinded by her irresistible charms.... She is the goddess of sexuality, and *Cannibal Flower* is her haunting siren song."—Michael Perkins
$4.95/72-6

RHINOCEROS BOOKS

MICHAEL PERKINS

EVIL COMPANIONS
Set in New York City during the tumultuous waning years of the Sixties, *Evil Companions* has been hailed as "a frightening classic." A young couple explores the nether reaches of the erotic unconscious in a shocking confrontation with the extremes of passion. With a new introduction by science fiction legend Samuel R. Delany. $6.95/3067-9

AN ANTHOLOGY OF CLASSIC ANONYMOUS EROTIC WRITING
Michael Perkins, acclaimed authority on erotic literature, has collected the very best passages from the world's erotic writing—especially for Rhino*ceros* readers. "Anonymous" is one of the most infamous bylines in publishing history—and these steamy excerpts show why! An incredible smorgasbord of forbidden delights culled from some of the most famous titles in the history of erotic literature. $6.95/140-3

THE SECRET RECORD: Modern Erotic Literature
Michael Perkins surveys the field with authority and unique insight. Updated and revised to include the latest trends, tastes, and developments in this misunderstood and maligned genre. $6.95/3039-3

HELEN HENLEY

ENTER WITH TRUMPETS
Helen Henley was told that women just don't write about sex—much less the taboos she was so interested in exploring. So Henley did it alone, flying in the face of "tradition," by producing *Enter With Trumpets*, a touching tale of arousal and devotion in one couple's kinky relationship. $6.95/197-7

PHILIP JOSE FARMER

FLESH
Space Commander Stagg explored the galaxies for 800 years. Upon his return, the hero Stagg is made the centerpiece of an incredible public ritual—one that will repeatedly take him to the heights of ecstasy, and inexorably drag him toward the depths of hell. $6.95/303-1

A FEAST UNKNOWN
"Sprawling, brawling, shocking, suspenseful, hilarious..."
—Theodore Sturgeon
Farmer's supreme anti-hero returns. "I was conceived and born in 1888." Slowly, Lord Grandrith—armed with the belief that he is the son of Jack the Ripper—tells the story of his remarkable and unbridled life. His story begins with his discovery of the secret of immortality.... $6.95/276-0

THE IMAGE OF THE BEAST
Herald Childe has seen Hell, glimpsed its horror in an act of sexual mutilation. Childe must now find and destroy an inhuman predator through the streets of a polluted and decadent Los Angeles of the future. One clue after another leads Childe to an inescapable realization about the nature of sex and evil.... $6.95/166-7

LEOPOLD VON SACHER-MASOCH

VENUS IN FURS
This classic 19th century novel is the first uncompromising exploration of the dominant/submissive relationship in literature. The alliance of Severin and Wanda epitomizes Sacher-Masoch's dark obsession with a cruel, controlling goddess and the urges that drive the man held in her thrall. Includes the letters exchanged between Sacher-Masoch and Emilie Mataja, an aspiring writer he sought as the avatar of his forbidden desires. $6.95/3089-X

RHINOCEROS BOOKS

SOPHIE GALLEYMORE BIRD
MANEATER
Through a bizarre act of creation, a man attains the "perfect" lover—by all appearances a beautiful, sensuous woman, but in reality something far darker. Once brought to life she will accept no mate, seeking instead the prey that will sate her hunger for vengeance. A biting take on the war of the sexes, this debut goes for the jugular of the "perfect woman" myth. $6.95/103-9

TUPPY OWENS
SENSATIONS
A piece of porn history. Tuppy Owens tells the unexpurgated story of the making of *Sensations*—the first big-budget sex flick. Originally commissioned to appear in book form after the release of the film in 1975, *Sensations* is finally released under Masquerade's stylish Rhino*ceros* imprint. $6.95/3081-4

SAMUEL R. DELANY
THE MAD MAN
"The latest novel from Hugo- and Nebula-winning science fiction writer and critic Delany...reads like a pornographic reflection of Peter Ackroyd's *Chatterton* or A. S. Byatt's *Possession*.... The pornographic element... becomes more than simple shock or titillation, though, as Delany develops an insightful dichotomy between [his protagonist]'s two worlds: the one of cerebral philosophy and dry academia, the other of heedless, 'impersonal' obsessive sexual extremism. When these worlds finally collide...the novel achieves a surprisingly satisfying resolution...." —*Publishers Weekly*

The mass market debut of Samuel R. Delany's most provocative novel. For his thesis, graduate student John Marr researches the life and work of the brilliant Timothy Hasler: a philosopher whose career was cut tragically short over a decade earlier. On another front, Marr finds himself increasingly drawn toward more shocking, depraved sexual entanglements with the homeless men of his neighborhood, until it begins to seem that Hasler's death might hold some key to his own life as a gay man in the age of AIDS. $8.99/408-9

EQUINOX
The *Scorpion* has sailed the seas in a quest for every possible pleasure. Her crew is a collection of the young, the twisted, the insatiable. A drifter comes into their midst and is taken on a fantastic journey to the darkest, most dangerous sexual extremes—until he is finally a victim to their boundless appetites. $6.95/157-8

DANIEL VIAN
ILLUSIONS
Two tales of danger and desire in Berlin on the eve of WWII. From private homes to lurid cafés, passion is exposed and explored in stark contrast to the brutal violence of the time. A singularly arousing volume; two shockingly sexy tales examining a remarkably decadent age.. $6.95/3074-1

PERSUASIONS
"The stockings are drawn tight by the suspender belt, tight enough to be stretched to the limit just above the middle part of her thighs..." A double novel, including the classics *Adagio* and *Gabriela and the General*, this volume traces desire around the globe. Two classics of international lust!

$6.95/183-7

RHINOCEROS BOOKS

ANDREI CODRESCU

THE REPENTANCE OF LORRAINE

"One of our most prodigiously talented and magical writers."
—*NYT Book Review*

By the acclaimed author of *The Hole in the Flag* and *The Blood Countess*. An aspiring writer, a professor's wife, a secretary, gold anklets, Maoists, Roman harlots—and more—swirl through this spicy tale of a harried quest for a mythic artifact. Written when the author was a young man, this lusty yarn was inspired by the heady days of the Sixties. Includes a new Introduction by the author, painting a portrait of *Lorraine*'s creation. $6.95/329-5

LIESEL KULIG

LOVE IN WARTIME

Madeleine knew that the handsome SS officer was a dangerous man, but she was just a cabaret singer in Nazi-occupied Paris, trying to survive in a perilous time. When Josef fell in love with her, he discovered that a beautiful and amoral woman can sometimes be more dangerous than a highly skilled soldier.
$6.95/3044-X

MASQUERADE BOOKS

POINT OF VIEW — *Martine Glowinski*

After her divorce, one woman experiences the ultimate erotic awakening. With the assistance of her new, unexpectedly kinky lover, she discovers and explores her exhibitionist tendencies—until there is virtually nothing she won't do before the horny audiences her man arranges! Unabashed acting out for the sophisticated voyeur. $6.50/433-X

A HARLOT OF VENUS — *Richard McGowan*

A highly fanciful, epic tale of lust on Mars! Cavortia—the most famous and sought-after courtesan in the cosmopolitan city of Venus—finds love and much more during her adventures with some of the most remarkable characters in recent erotic fiction. An exquisitely erotic adult fable. $6.50/425-9

THE ARCHITECTURE OF DESIRE — *M. Orlando*

Introduction by Richard Manton. Two novels in one special volume! In *The Hotel Justine*, an elite clientele is afforded the opportunity to have any and all desires satisfied. *The Villa Sin* is inherited by a beautiful but discontented woman who soon realizes that the legacy of the ancestral estate includes bizarre erotic ceremonies and sexual extremism. Two pieces of prime real estate. $6.50/490-9

KISS ME, KATHERINE — *Chet Rothwell*

Husband—or slave? Beautiful Katherine can hardly believe her luck. Not only is she married to the charming and oh-so-agreeable Nelson, she's free to live out all her erotic fantasies with other men as well. Katherine has discovered Nelson to be far more devoted than the average spouse—and the duo soon begin exploring a relationship that could prove more demanding than marriage! $5.95/410-0

THE STONED APOCALYPSE — *Marco Vassi*

"Marco Vassi is our champion: sexual energist." —*VLS*

During his lifetime, Marco Vassi was hailed as America's premier erotic writer and most worthy successor to Henry Miller. His work was praised by writers as diverse as Gore Vidal and Norman Mailer, and his reputation was worldwide. *The Stoned Apocalypse* is Vassi's autobiography; chronicling a cross-country trip on America's erotic byways, it offers a rare glimpse of a generation's sexual imagination. $5.95/401-1/mass market

MASQUERADE BOOKS

TABITHA'S TEASE *Robin Wilde*
When poor Robin arrives at The Valentine Academy, he finds himself subject to the tortuous teasing of Tabitha—the Academy's most notoriously domineering co-ed. But Tabitha is pledge-mistress of a secret sorority dedicated to enslaving young men. Robin finds himself the utterly helpless (and wildly excited) captive of Tabitha & Company's weird desires! $5.95/387-2

PIRATE'S SLAVE *Erica Bronte*
Lovely young Erica is stranded in a country where lust knows no bounds. Desperate to escape, she finds herself trading her firm, luscious body to any and all men willing and able to help her. Her adventure has its ups and downs, ins and outs—all to the undeniable pleasure of lusty Erica! $5.95/376-7

HELLFIRE *Charles G. Wood*
A vicious murderer is running amok in New York's sexual underground—and Nick O'Shay, a virile detective with the NYPD, plunges deep into the case. He soon becomes embroiled in an elusive world of fleshly extremes, hunting a madman seeking to purge America with fire and blood sacrifices.

"[Wood] betrays a photographer's eye for tableau and telling detail in his evocation of the larger-than-life figures of the late-'70s to mid-'80s sexual demimonde." —David Aaron Clark, author of *The Wet Forever*
$5.95/358-9

THE MISTRESS OF CASTLE ROHMENSTADT
Olivia M. Ravensworth
Lovely Katherine inherits a secluded European castle from a mysterious relative. Upon arrival she discovers, much to her delight, that the castle is a haven of sensual pleasure. Katherine learns to shed her inhibitions and enjoy her new home's many delights. $5.95/372-4

LA DOMME: A DOMINATRIX ANTHOLOGY *Edited by Claire Baeder*
A steamy smorgasbord of female domination! Erotic literature has long been filled with heartstopping portraits of domineering women, and now the most memorable come together in one beautifully brutal volume. $5.95/366-X

THE GEEK *Tiny Alice*
"An adventure novel told by a sex-bent male mini-pygmy. This is an accomplishment of which anybody may be proud."—Philip José Farmer

The Geek is told from the point of view of, well, a chicken, who reports on the various perversities he witnesses as part of a traveling carnival. When a gang of renegade lesbians kidnaps Chicken and his geek, all hell breaks loose. A strange tale, filled with outrageous erotic oddities. $5.95/341-4

SEX ON THE NET *Charisse van der Lyn*
Electrifying erotica from one of the Internet's hottest and most widely read authors. Encounters of all kinds—straight, lesbian, dominant/submissive and all sorts of extreme passions—are explored in thrilling detail. $5.95/399-6

BEAUTY OF THE BEAST *Carole Remy*
A shocking tell-all, written from the point-of-view of a prize-winning reporter. And what reporting she does! All the secrets of an uninhibited life are revealed, and each lusty tableau is painted in glowing colors. $5.95/332-5

NAUGHTY MESSAGE *Stanley Carten*
Wesley Arthur, a withdrawn computer engineer, discovers a lascivious message on his answering machine. Aroused beyond his wildest dreams by the unmentionable acts described, Wesley becomes obsessed with tracking down the woman behind the seductive voice. His search takes him through strip clubs, sex parolors and no-tell motels—and finally to his randy reward....
$5.95/333-3

MASQUERADE BOOKS

The Marquis de Sade's JULIETTE *David Aaron Clark*
The Marquis de Sade's infamous Juliette returns—and emerges as the most perverse and destructive nightstalker modern New York will ever know. Under this domina's tutelage, two beautiful women come to know torture's bizarre attractions as they grapple with the price of Juliette's immortality.
Praise for David Aaron Clark:
"David Aaron Clark has delved into one of the most sensationalistically taboo aspects of eros, sadomasochism, and produced a novel of unmistakable literary imagination and artistic value." —Carlo McCormick, *Paper*
$5.95/240-X

NADIA *Anonymous*
Follow the delicious but neglected Nadia as she works to wring every drop of pleasure out of life—despite an unhappy marriage. A classic title providing a peek into the secret sexual lives of another time and place. $5.95/267-1

THE STORY OF A VICTORIAN MAID *Nigel McParr*
What were the Victorians really like? Chances are, no one believes they were as stuffy as their Queen, but who would have imagined such unbridled libertines! Follow her from exploit to smutty exploit! $5.95/241-8

CARRIE'S STORY *Molly Weatherfield*
"I had been Jonathan's slave for about a year when he told me he wanted to sell me at an auction. I wasn't in any condition to respond when he told me this..." Desire and depravity run rampant in this story of uncompromising mastery and irrevocable submission. $5.95/444-5

CHARLY'S GAME *Bren Flemming*
A rich woman's gullible daughter has run off with one of the toughest leather dykes in town—and sexy P.I. Charly is hired to lure the girl back. One by one, wise and wicked women ensnare one another in their lusty nets! $4.95/221-3

ANDREA AT THE CENTER *J.P. Kansas*
Lithe and lovely young Andrea is, without warning, whisked away to a distant retreat. There she is introduced to the ways of the Center, and soon becomes quite friendly with its other inhabitants—all of whom are learning to abandon restraint in their pursuit of the deepest sexual satisfaction. $5.95/324-4

ASK ISADORA *Isadora Alman*
Six years' worth of Isadora Alman's syndicated columns on sex and relationships. Alman's been called a "hip Dr. Ruth," and a "sexy Dear Abby," based upon the wit and pertinence of her advice. Today's world is more perplexing than ever—and Alman can help untangle the most personal of knots. $4.95/61-0

STASI SLUT *Anthony Bobarzynski*
Adina lives in East Germany, where she meets a group of ruthless and corrupt STASI agents who use her for their own perverse gratification—until she uses her talents and attractions in a final bid for total freedom! $4.95/3050-4

LOUISE BELHAVEL
FRAGRANT ABUSES
The saga of Clara and Iris continues as the now-experienced girls enjoy themselves with a new circle of worldly friends whose imaginations match their own. Perversity follows the lusty ladies around the globe! $4.95/88-2

TITIAN BERESFORD
THE WICKED HAND
With a special Introduction by *Leg Show*'s Dian Hanson. A collection of fanciful fetishistic tales featuring the absolute subjugation of men by lovely, domineering women. From Japan and Germany to the American heartland—these stories uncover the other side of the "weaker sex." $5.95/343-0

MASQUERADE BOOKS

CINDERELLA
Beresford triumphs again with this intoxicating tale, filled with castle dungeons and tightly corseted ladies-in-waiting, naughty viscounts and impossibly cruel masturbatrixes—nearly every conceivable method of erotic torture is explored and described in lush, vivid detail. $4.95/305-8

JUDITH BOSTON
Young Edward would have been lucky to get the stodgy old companion he thought his parents had hired for him. Instead, an exquisite woman arrives at his door, and Edward finds his compulsively lewd behavior never goes unpunished by the unflinchingly severe Judith Boston! $4.95/273-6

NINA FOXTON
An aristocrat finds herself bored by run-of-the-mill amusements for "ladies of good breeding." Instead of taking tea with proper gentlemen, naughty Nina "milks" them of their most private essences. No man ever says "No" to Nina! $5.95/443-7

A TITIAN BERESFORD READER
Wild dominatrixes, perverse masochists, and mesmerizing detail are the hallmarks of the Beresford tale—and encountered here in abundance. The very best scenarios from all of Beresford's bestsellers. $4.95/114-4

CHINA BLUE

KUNG FU NUNS
"She lifted me out of the chair and sat me down on top of the table. She then lifted her skirt. The sight of her perfect legs clad in white stockings and a petite garter belt further mesmerized me...." China Blue returns! $4.95/3031-8

LYN DAVENPORT

DOVER ISLAND
Off the coast of Oregon, Dr. David Kelly has planted the seeds of his dream—a Corporal Punishment Resort. Soon, many people from varied walks of life descend upon this isolated retreat, intent on fulfilling their every desire. Included in this elite gathering is Marcy Harris, who will prove the perfect partner for the lonely but lustful Doctor.... $5.95/384-8

TESSA'S HOLIDAYS
Tessa's lusty lover, Grant, makes sure that each of her holidays is filled with the type of sensual adventure most young women only dream about. What will her insatiable man dream up next? Only he knows—and he keeps his secrets until the lovely Tessa is ready to explode with desire! $5.95/377-5

THE GUARDIAN
Felicia grew up under the tutelage of the lash—and she learned her lessons well. Sir Rodney Wentworth has long searched for a woman capable of fulfilling his cruel desires, and after learning of Felicia's talents, sends for her. Upon arrival in his home, Felicia discovers that the "position" offered her is delightfully different than anything she could have expected! $5.95/371-6

P. N. DEDEAUX

THE NOTHING THINGS
Beta Beta Rho—highly exclusive and widely honored—has taken on a new group of pledges. The five women will be put through the most grueling of ordeals, and punished severely for any shortcomings—much to everyone's delight! $5.95/404-6

TENDER BUNS
In a fashionable Canadian suburb, Marc Merlin indulges his yen for punishment with an assortment of the town's most desirable and willing women. Things come to a rousing climax at a party planned to cater to just those whims Marc is most able to satisfy.... $5.95/396-1

MASQUERADE BOOKS

AKBAR DEL PIOMBO
SKIRTS
Randy Mr. Edward Champdick enters high society—and a whole lot more—in his quest for ultimate satisfaction. For it seems that once Mr. Champdick rises to the occasion, nothing can bring him down. $4.95/115-2

DUKE COSIMO
A kinky romp played out against the boudoirs, bathrooms and ballrooms of the European nobility, who seem to do nothing all day except each other. The lifestyles of the rich and licentious are revealed in all their glory. $4.95/3052-0

A CRUMBLING FAÇADE
The return of that incorrigible rogue, Henry Pike, who continues his pursuit of sex, fair or otherwise, in the most elegant homes of the most debauched aristocrats. No one can resist the irrepressible Pike! $4.95/3043-1

PAULA
This canny seductress tests the mettle of every man who comes under her spell—and every man does! Lovely Paula proves herself capable of devouring any man unable to match her wanton ways. $4.95/3036-9

ROBERT DESMOND
THE SWEETEST FRUIT
Connie is determined to seduce and destroy the devoted Father Chadcroft. She corrupts the unsuspecting priest into forsaking all that he holds sacred, destroys his parish, and slyly manipulates him with her smoldering looks and hypnotic aura. This Magdalene drags her unsuspecting prey into a hell of unbridled lust.
$4.95/95-5

MICHAEL DRAX
SILK AND STEEL
"He let his robe fall to the floor. She could offer no resistance as the shadowy figure knelt before her, gazing down upon her. Why would she resist? This was what she wanted all along...." $4.95/3032-6

OBSESSIONS
Victoria is determined to become a model by sexually ensnaring the powerful people who control the fashion industry: Paige, who finds herself compelled to watch Victoria's conquests; and Pietro and Alex, who take turns and then join in for a sizzling threesome. $4.95/3012-1

LIZBETH DUSSEAU
TRINKETS
"Her bottom danced on the air, pert and fully round. It would take punishment well, he thought." A luscious woman submits to an artist's every whim—becoming the sexual trinket he had always desired. $5.95/246-9

SPANISH HOLIDAY
She didn't know what to make of Sam Jacobs. He was undoubtedly the most remarkable man she'd ever met.... Lauren didn't mean to fall in love with the enigmatic Sam, but a once-in-a-lifetime European vacation gives her all the evidence she needs that this hot man might be the one for her.... $4.95/185-3

CAROLINE'S CONTRACT
After a life of repression, Caroline goes out on a limb. On the advice of a friend, she meets with the alluring Max Burton—a man more than willing to indulge her fantasies of domination and discipline. Caroline soon learns to love his ministrations—and agrees to a very *special* arrangement, sure to teach her all she needs to know of submission.... $4.95/122-5

MASQUERADE BOOKS

SARA H. FRENCH

MASTER OF TIMBERLAND
A tale of sexual slavery at the ultimate paradise resort. One of our bestselling titles, this trek to Timberland has ignited passions the world over—and stands poised to become one of modern erotica's legendary tales. $5.95/327-9

RETURN TO TIMBERLAND
It's time for a trip back to Timberland, the world's most frenzied sexual resort! Prepare for a vacation filled with delicious decadence, as each and every visitor is serviced by unimaginably talented submissives. These nubile maidens are determined to make this the raunchiest camp-out ever—and succeed with the help of their rampant campers! The astonishing sequel to a perennial best-seller. $5.95/257-4

SARAH JACKSON

SANCTUARY
Tales from the Middle Ages. *Sanctuary* explores both the unspeakable debauchery of court life and the unimaginable privations of monastic solitude, leading the voracious and the virtuous on a collision course that brings history to throbbing life. $5.95/318-X

JOCELYN JOYCE

PRIVATE LIVES
The lecherous habits of the illustrious make for a sizzling tale of French erotic life. A widow has a craving for a young busboy; he's sleeping with a rich businessman's wife; her husband is minding his sex business elsewhere! Scandalous sexual entanglements run throughout this tale of upper crust lust! $4.95/309-0

CANDY LIPS
The world of publishing serves as the backdrop for one woman's pursuit of sexual satisfaction. From a fiery femme fatale to a voracious Valentino, she takes her pleasure where she can find it. Luckily for her, it's most often found between the legs of the most licentious lovers! $4.95/182-9

KIM'S PASSION
The life of an insatiable seductress. Kim leaves India for London, where she quickly takes on the task of bedding every woman in sight! $4.95/162-4

CAROUSEL
A young American woman leaves her husband when she discovers he is having an affair with their maid. She then becomes the sexual plaything of various Parisian voluptuaries. Wild sex, low morals! $4.95/3051-2

SABINE
There is no one who can refuse her once she casts her spell; no lover can do anything less than give up his whole life for her. Great men and empires fall at her feet; but she is haughty, distracted, impervious. It is the eve of WWII, and Sabine must find a new lover equal to her talents. $4.95/3046-6

THE WILD HEART
A luxury hotel is the setting for this artful web of sex, desire, and love. A newlywed sees sex as a duty, while her hungry husband tries to awaken her to its tender joys. A Parisian entertains wealthy guests for the love of money. Each episode provides a new variation in this lusty Grand Hotel! $4.95/3007-5

JADE EAST
Laura, passive and passionate, follows her husband Emilio to Hong Kong. He gives her to Wu Li, a connoisseur of sexual perversions, who passes her on to Madeleine, a flamboyant lesbian. Madeleine's friends make Laura the centerpiece in Hong Kong's infamous underground orgies. $4.95/60-2

MASQUERADE BOOKS

THE JAZZ AGE
The time: the Roaring Twenties. A young attorney becomes suspicious of his mistress, while his wife has a fling with a lesbian lover. *The Jazz Age* is a romp of erotic realism from the heyday of the speakeasy. $4.95/48-3

AMARANTHA KNIGHT

THE DARKER PASSIONS READER
The very best moments from Amarantha Knight's phenomenally popular Darker Passions series. Here are the most eerily erotic passages from her acclaimed sexual reworkings of *Dracula*, *Frankenstein*, *Dr. Jeykll & Mr. Hyde* and *The Fall of the House of Usher*. Be prepared for more than a few thrills and chills from this arousing sampler. $6.50/432-1

THE DARKER PASSIONS: *FRANKENSTEIN*
What if you could create a living, breathing human? What shocking acts could it be taught to perform, to desire, to love? Find out what pleasures await those who play God.... $5.95/248-5

THE DARKER PASSIONS: *THE FALL OF THE HOUSE OF USHER*
The Master and Mistress of the house of Usher indulge in every form of decadence, and are intent on initiating their guests into the many pleasures to be found in utter submission. $5.95/313-9

THE DARKER PASSIONS: *DR. JEKYLL AND MR. HYDE*
It is a story of incredible, frightening transformations achieved through mysterious experiments. Now, Amarantha Knight explores the steamy possibilities of a tale where no one is quite who—or what—they seem. Victorian bedrooms explode with hidden demons! $4.95/227-2

THE DARKER PASSIONS: *DRACULA*
The infamous erotic retelling of the Vampire legend.
"Well-written and imaginative, Amarantha Knight gives fresh impetus to this myth, taking us through the sexual and sadistic scenes with details that keep us reading.... A classic in itself has been added to the shelves." —*Divinity* $5.95/326-0

ALIZARIN LAKE

SEX ON DOCTOR'S ORDERS
A chronicle of selfless devotion to mankind! Beth, a nubile young nurse, uses her considerable skills to further medical science by offering incomparable and insatiable assistance in the gathering of important specimens. No man leaves naughty Nurse Beth's station without surrendering exactly what she needs! A guaranteed cure for all types of fever. $5.95/402-X

THE EROTIC ADVENTURES OF HARRY TEMPLE
Harry Temple's memoirs chronicle his amorous adventures from his initiation at the hands of insatiable sirens, through his stay at a house of hot repute, to his encounters with a chastity-belted nympho! $4.95/127-6

MORE EROTIC ADVENTURES OF HARRY TEMPLE
Harry Temple's lustful adventures continue. This time he begins his amorous pursuits by deflowering the ample and eager Aurora. Harry soon discovers that his little protégée is more than able to match him at every lascivious game and very willing to display her own talents. $4.95/67-X

CLARA
The mysterious death of a beautiful woman leads her old boyfriend on a harrowing journey of discovery. His search uncovers a woman on a quest for deeper and more unusual sensations, each more shocking than the one before. $4.95/80-7

MASQUERADE BOOKS

DIARY OF AN ANGEL
A long-forgotten diary tells the story of angelic Victoria, lured into a secret life of unimaginable depravity. "I am like a fly caught in a spider's web, a helpless and voiceless victim of their every whim." $4.95/71-8

MISS HIGH HEELS
It was a delightful punishment few men dared to dream of. Who could have predicted how far it would go? Forced by his sisters to dress and behave like a proper lady, Dennis finds he enjoys life as Denise much more! $4.95/3066-0

PAUL LITTLE

ALL THE WAY
Two excruciating novels from Paul Little in one hot volume! *Going All the Way* features an unhappy man who tries to purge himself of the memory of his lover with a series of quirky and uninhibited lovers. *Pushover* tells the story of a serial spanker and his celebrated exploits. $6.95/509-3

THE DISCIPLINE OF ODETTE
Odette's was sure marriage would rescue her from her family's "corrections." To her horror, she discovers that her beloved has also been raised on discipline. A shocking erotic coupling! $5.95/334-1

THE PRISONER
Judge Black has built a secret room below a penitentiary, where he sentences the prisoners to hours of exhibition and torment while his friends watch. Judge Black's House of Corrections is equipped with one purpose in mind: to administer his own brand of rough justice! $5.95/330-9

TUTORED IN LUST
This tale of the initiation and instruction of a carnal college co-ed and her fellow students unlocks the sex secrets of the classroom. Books take a back seat to secret societies and their bizarre ceremonies in this story of students with an unquenchable thirst for knowledge! $4.95/78-5

TEARS OF THE INQUISITION
The incomparable Paul Little delivers a staggering account of pleasure and punishment. *"There was a tickling inside her as her nervous system reminded her she was ready for sex. But before her was...the Inquisitor!"* $4.95/146-2

DOUBLE NOVEL
Two of Paul Little's bestselling novels in one spellbinding volume! *The Metamorphosis of Lisette Joyaux* tells the story of an innocent young woman initiated into a new world of lesbian lusts. *The Story of Monique* reveals the sexual rituals that beckon the ripe and willing Monique. $4.95/86-6

CHINESE JUSTICE AND OTHER STORIES
The story of the excruciating pleasures and delicious punishments inflicted on foreigners under the leaders of the Boxer Rebellion. Each foreign woman is brought before the authorities and grilled. Scandalous deeds! $4.95/153-5

CAPTIVE MAIDENS
Three beautiful young women find themselves powerless against the wealthy, debauched landowners of 1824 England. They are banished to a sexual slave colony, and corrupted by every imaginable perversion. Soon, they come to crave the treatment of their unrelenting captors. $5.95/440-2

SLAVE ISLAND
A leisure cruise is waylaid, finding itself in the domain of Lord Henry Philbrock, a sadistic genius. The ship's passengers are kidnapped and spirited to his island prison, where the women are trained to accommodate the most bizarre sexual cravings of the rich, the famous, the pampered and the perverted. An incredible best-seller. $5.95/441-0

MASQUERADE BOOKS

MARY LOVE
MASTERING MARY SUE
Mary Sue is a rich nymphomaniac whose husband is determined to pervert her, declare her mentally incompetent, and gain control of her fortune. He brings her to a castle where, to Mary Sue's delight, she is unleashed for a veritable sex-fest! $5.95/351-1

THE BEST OF MARY LOVE
Mary Love leaves no coupling untried and no extreme unexplored in these scandalous selections from *Mastering Mary Sue, Ecstasy on Fire, Vice Park Place, Wanda,* and *Naughtier at Night.* $4.95/3099-7

JOHN NORMAN
TARNSMAN OF GOR
This legendary—and controversial—series returns! *Tarnsman* finds Tarl Cabot transported to Counter-Earth, better known as Gor. He must quickly accustom himself to the ways of this world, including the caste system which exalts some as Priest-Kings or Warriors, and debases others as slaves. A spectacular world unfolds in this first volume of John Norman's million-selling Gorean series. $6.95/486-0

OUTLAW OF GOR
The Strange History of Counter-Earth continues! In this volume, Tarl Cabot returns to Gor, where he might reclaim both his woman and his role of Warrior. But he discovers that his name, his city and the names of those he loves are unspeakable now. He has become an outlaw, and must discover his new purpose on this strange planet, where danger stalks the outcast, and simple answers have their price.... $6.95/487-9

RACHEL PEREZ
ODD WOMEN
These women are lots of things: sexy, smart, innocent, tough—some even say odd. But who cares, when their combined ass-ettes are so sweet! There's not a moral in sight as an assortment of Sapphic sirens proves once and for all that comely ladies come best in pairs. $4.95/123-3

AFFINITIES
"Kelsy had a liking for cool upper-class blondes, the long-legged girls from Lake Forest and Winnetka who came into the city to cruise the lesbian bars on Halsted, looking for breathless ecstasies...." A scorching tale of lesbian libidos unleashed, from a writer more than capable of exploring every nuance of female passion in vivid detail. $4.95/113-6

CHARLOTTE ROSE
WOMEN AT WORK
Hot stories devoted to the working woman! From a lonesome cowgirl to a supercharged public relations exec, these women know the best way to let off steam after a tough day on the job. Includes "A Cowgirl's Passion," the story which ranked #1 on Dr. Ruth's list of favorite erotic stories for women! $4.95/3088-1

SYDNEY ST. JAMES
RIVE GAUCHE
Decadence and debauchery among the doomed artists in the Latin Quarter, Paris, circa 1920. Expatriate bohemians couple with abandon—before eventually abandoning their ambitions amidst the intoxicating temptations waiting to be indulged in every bedroom. $5.95/317-1

MASQUERADE BOOKS

THE HIGHWAYWOMAN
A young filmmaker making a documentary about the life of the notorious English highwaywoman, Bess Ambrose, becomes obsessed with her mysterious subject. It seems that Bess touched more than hearts—and plundered the treasures of every man and maiden she met on the way. $4.95/174-8

GARDEN OF DELIGHT
A vivid account of sexual awakening that follows an innocent but insatiably curious young woman's journey from the furtive, forbidden joys of dormitory life to the unabashed carnality of the wild world. $4.95/3058-X

ALEXANDER TROCCHI

THONGS
"...In Spain, life is cheap, from that glittering tragedy in the bullring to the quick thrust of the stiletto in a narrow street in a Barcelona slum. No, this death would not have called for further comment had it not been for one striking fact. The naked woman had met her end in a way he had never seen before—a way that had enormous sexual significance. My God, she had been..." $4.95/217-5

HELEN AND DESIRE
Helen Seferis' flight from the oppressive village of her birth became a sexual tour of a harsh world. From brothels in Sydney to harems in Algiers, Helen chronicles her adventures fully in her diary. Each encounter is examined in the scorching and uncensored diary of the sensual Helen! $4.95/3093-8

THE CARNAL DAYS OF HELEN SEFERIS
P.I. Anthony Harvest is assigned to save Helen Seferis, a beautiful Australian who has been abducted. Following clues in her explicit diary of adventures, he pursues the lovely, doomed Helen—the ultimate sexual prize. $4.95/3086-5

WHITE THIGHS
A fantasy of obsession from a modern erotic master. This is the story of Saul and his sexual fixation on the beautiful, tormented Anna. Their scorching passion leads to murder and madness every time. $4.95/3009-1

MARCUS VAN HELLER

TERROR
Another shocking exploration of lust by the author of the ever-popular *Adam & Eve*. Set in Paris during the Algerian War, *Terror* explores the place of sexual passion in a world drunk on violence. $5.95/247-7

KIDNAP
Private Investigator Harding is called in to investigate a mysterious kidnapping case involving the rich and powerful. Along the way he has the pleasure of "interrogating" an exotic dancer named Jeanne and a beautiful English reporter, as he finds himself enmeshed in the crime underworld. $4.95/90-4

LUSCIDIA WALLACE

KATY'S AWAKENING
Katy thinks she's been rescued after a terrible car wreck. Little does she suspect that she's been ensnared by a ring of swingers, whose tastes run to domination and unimaginably depraved sex parties. With no means of escape, Katy becomes the newest initiate in this sick private club—much to her pleasure! $4.95/308-2

N. WHALLEN

TAU'TEVU
In a mysterious land, the statuesque and beautiful Vivian learns to subject herself to the hand of a mysterious man. He systematically helps her prove her own strength, and brings to life in her an unimagined sensual fire. But who is this man, who goes only by the name of Orpheo? $6.50/426-7

MASQUERADE BOOKS

COMPLIANCE
Fourteen stories exploring the pleasures of release. Characters from many walks of life learn to trust in the skills of others, only to experience the thrilling liberation of submission. Here are the real joys to be found in some of the most forbidden sexual practices around.... $5.95/356-2

DON WINSLOW

SECRETS OF CHEATEM MANOR
Young Edward returns to his late father's estate, to find it being run by the majestic Lady Amanda Longleigh. Edward can hardly believe his luck—Lady Amanda is assisted by her two beautiful, lonely daughters, Catherine and Prudence. What the randy young man soon comes to realize is the love of discipline that all three beauties share. One young man at the mercy of three cruel goddesses! $6.50/434-8

KATERINA IN CHARGE
When invited to a country retreat by a mysterious couple, the two randy young ladies can hardly resist! But do they have any idea what they're in for? Whatever the case, the imperious Katerina will make her desires known very soon—and demand that they be fulfilled.... $5.95/409-7

THE MANY PLEASURES OF IRONWOOD
Seven lovely young women are employed by The Ironwood Sportsmen's Club A small and exclusive club with seven carefully selected sexual connoisseurs, Ironwood is dedicated to the relentless pursuit of sensual pleasure. $5.95/310-4

CLAIRE'S GIRLS
You knew when she walked by that she was something special. She was one of Claire's girls, a woman carefully dressed and groomed to fill a role, to capture a look, to fit an image crafted by the sophisticated proprietress of an exclusive escort agency. High-class whores blow the roof off! $5.95/442-9

THE MASQUERADE READERS

THE COMPLETE EROTIC READER
The very best in erotic writing is brought together in a thoroughly wicked collection sure to stimulate even the most jaded and "sophisticated" palates. $4.95/3063-6

INTIMATE PLEASURES
Forbidden liaisons, bizarre public displays of carnality and insatiable cravings abound in these excerpts from six of our very bestselling erotic novels. $4.95/38-6

THE VELVET TONGUE
An orgy of oral gratification! *The Velvet Tongue* celebrates the most mouth-watering, lip-smacking, tongue-twisting action. A feast of fellatio and *soixante-neuf* awaits readers of excellent taste at this steamy suck-fest. $4.95/3029-6

A MASQUERADE READER
A sizzling sampler Strict lessons are learned at the hand of *The English Governess*. Scandalous confessions are found in *The Diary of an Angel*, and the story of a woman whose desires drove her to the ultimate sacrifice in *Thongs* completes the collection. $4.95/84-X

THE CLASSIC COLLECTION

PROTESTS, PLEASURES, RAPTURES
Invited for an allegedly quiet weekend at a country vicarage, a young woman is stunned to find herself surrounded by shocking acts of sexual sadism. Soon, her curiosity is piqued, and she begins to explore her own capacities for cruelty—leading to an all-out search for an appropriately punishable partner. $5.95/400-3

MASQUERADE BOOKS

THE YELLOW ROOM
Two legendary erotic stories. The "yellow room" holds the secrets of lust, lechery, and the lash. There, bare-bottomed, spread-eagled, and open to the world, demure Alice Darvell soon learns to love her lickings. Even more exciting is the second torrid tale of hot heiress Rosa Coote and her adventures in punishment and pleasure. Two feverishly erotic descents into utter depravity!
$5.95/378-3

SCHOOL DAYS IN PARIS
The rapturous chronicles of a well-spent youth! Few Universities provide the profound and pleasurable lessons one learns in after-hours study—particularly if one is young and available, and lucky enough to have Paris as a playground. A stimulating look at the pursuits of young adulthood. $5.95/325-2

MAN WITH A MAID
The adventures of Jack and Alice have delighted readers for eight decades! A classic of its genre, *Man with a Maid* tells an outrageous tale of desire, revenge, and submission. This tale qualifies as one of the world's most popular adult novels—with over 200,000 copies in print! $4.95/307-4

MAN WITH A MAID II
Jack's back! With the assistance of the perverse Alice, he embarks again on a trip through every erotic extreme. Jack leaves no one unsatisfied—least of all, himself—and Alice is always certain to outdo herself in her capacity to corrupt and control. An incendiary sequel! $4.95/3071-7

MAN WITH A MAID: The Conclusion
The final chapter in the epic saga of lust that has thrilled readers for decades. The adulterous woman who is corrected with enthusiasm and the maid who receives grueling guidance are just two who benefit from these lessons! Don't miss this conclusion to erotica's most famous tale. $4.95/3013-X

CONFESSIONS OF A CONCUBINE III: PLEASURE'S PRISONER
Filled with pulse-pounding excitement—including a daring escape from the harem and an encounter with an unspeakable sadist—*Pleasure's Prisoner* adds an unforgettable chapter to this thrilling confessional. $5.95/357-0

CONFESSIONS OF A CONCUBINE II: HAREM SLAVE
The concubinage continues, as the true pleasures and privileges of the harem are revealed. For the first time, readers are invited behind the veils that hide uninhibited, unimaginable pleasures from the world.... $4.95/226-4

INITIATION RITES
Every naughty detail of a young woman's breaking in! Under the thorough tutelage of the perverse Miss Clara Birchem, Julia learns her wicked lessons well. During the course of her amorous studies, the resourceful young lady is joined by an assortment of lewd characters who contribute to her carnal education in unspeakble ways.... $4.95/120-9

TABLEAUX VIVANTS
Fifteen breathtaking tales of erotic passion. Upstanding ladies and gents soon adopt more comfortable positions, as wicked thoughts explode into sinfully scrumptious acts. Soon, no one is safe from the arrows of Eros run amuck!
$4.95/121-7

LADY F.
An uncensored tale of Victorian passions. Master Kidrodstock suffers deliciously at the hands of the stunningly cruel and sensuous Lady Flayskin—the only woman capable of taming his wayward impulses. A fevered chronicle of punishing passions. $4.95/102-0

MASQUERADE BOOKS

CLASSIC EROTIC BIOGRAPHIES

JENNIFER III
The further adventures of erotica's most daring heroine. Jennifer, the quintessential beautiful blonde, has a photographer's eye for detail—particularly details of the masculine variety! A raging nymphomaniac takes on all comers! $5.95/292-2

JENNIFER AGAIN
One of contemporary erotica's hottest characters returns, in a sequel sure to blow you away. Once again, the insatiable Jennifer seizes the day—and extracts from it every last drop of sensual pleasure! $4.95/220-5

JENNIFER
From the bedroom of an internationally famous—and notoriously insatiable—dancer to an uninhibited ashram, *Jennifer* traces the exploits of one thoroughly modern woman as she lustfully explores the limits of her own sexuality. $4.95/107-1

ROSEMARY LANE *J.D. Hall*
The ups, downs, ins and outs of lovely Rosemary Lane. Raised as the ward of Lord and Lady D'Arcy, after coming of age she discovers that her guardians' generosity is boundless—as they contribute to her carnal education! $4.95/3078-4

THE ROMANCES OF BLANCHE LA MARE
When Blanche loses her husband, it becomes clear she'll need a job. She sets her sights on the stage—and soon encounters a cast of lecherous characters intent on making her path to sucksess as hot and hard as possible! $4.95/101-2

THE AMERICAN COLLECTION

LUST *Palmiro Vicarion*
A wealthy and powerful man of leisure recounts his rise up the corporate ladder and his corresponding descent into debauchery. A tale of a classic scoundrel with an uncurbed appetite for sexual power! $4.95/82-3

WAYWARD *Peter Jason*
A mysterious countess hires a tour bus for an unusual vacation. Traveling through Europe's most notorious cities, she picks up friends, lovers, and acquaintances from every walk of life in pursuit of pleasure. $4.95/3004-0

DANCE HALL GIRLS
The dance hall in Modesto was a ruthless trap for women of all ages. They learned to dance under the tutelage of sexual professionals. So grateful were they for the attention, they opened their hearts and their legs! $4.95/44-0

FOR A FREE COPY OF THE COMPLETE MASQUERADE CATALOG,
MAIL THIS COUPON TO:
**MASQUERADE DIRECT/DEPT BMMQ66
801 SECOND AVENUE, NEW YORK, NY 10017
OR FAX TO 212 986-7355**
All transactions are strictly confidential and we never sell, give or trade any customer's name.

NAME _____

ADDRESS _____

CITY _____ STATE _____ ZIP _____

A RICHARD KASAK BOOK

MICHAEL FORD, EDITOR
HAPPILY EVER AFTER: EROTIC FAIRY TALES FOR MEN

A hefty volume of bedtime stories Mother Goose never thought to write down. Adapting some of childhood's most beloved tales for the adult gay reader, the contributors to *Happily Ever After* dig up the subtext of these hitherto "innocent" diversions—adding some surprises of their own along the way.
$12.95/450-X

CHARLES HENRI FORD & PARKER TYLER
THE YOUNG AND EVIL

"*The Young and Evil creates [its] generation as* This Side of Paradise *by Fitzgerald created his generation.*" —Gertrude Stein

"*The first candid, gloves-off account of more or less professional young homosexuals.*" —Louis Kronenberger, *New Republic*

Originally published in 1933, *The Young and Evil* was an immediate sensation due to its unprecedented portrayal of young gay artists living in New York's notorious Greenwich Village. From flamboyant drag balls to squalid bohemian flats, these characters followed love and art wherever it led them—with a frankness that had the novel banned for many years. $12.95/431-3

SHAR REDNOUR, EDITOR
VIRGIN TERRITORY

An anthology of writing by women about their first-time erotic experiences with other women. From the longings and ecstasies of awakening dykes to the sometimes awkward pleasures of sexual experimentation on the edge, each of these true stories reveals a different, radical perspective on one of the most traditional subjects around: virginity. $12.95/457-7

HEATHER FINDLAY, EDITOR
A MOVEMENT OF EROS: 25 Years of Lesbian Erotica

One of the most scintillating overviews of lesbian erotic writing ever published. Heather Findlay has assembled a roster of stellar talents, each represented by their best work. Tracing the course of the genre from its pre-Stonewall roots to its current renaissance, Findlay examines such diverse talents as Jewelle Gomez, Chrystos, Pat Califia and Linda Smukler, placing them within the context of lesbian community and politics. $12.95/421-6

MICHAEL BRONSKI, EDITOR
TAKING LIBERTIES: Gay Male Essays on Politics, Culture and Sex

"*Taking Liberties offers undeniable proof of a heady, sophisticated, diverse new culture of gay intellectual debate. I cannot recommend it too highly.*" —Christopher Bram

Taking Liberties brings together some of the most divergent views on the state of contemporary gay male culture published in recent years. Michael Bronski, himself a widely published and respected gay cultural critic, here presents some of the community's foremost essayists weighing in on such slippery topics as outing, masculine identity, pornography, the pedophile movement, community definition, political strategy—and much more. $12.95/456-9

FLASHPOINT: Gay Male Sexual Writing

A collection of the most compelling, provocative testaments to gay eros. Longtime cultural critic Michael Bronski (*Culture Clash: The Making of Gay Sensibility*) presents over twenty of the genre's best writers, exploring areas such as Enlightenment, Violence, True Life Adventures and more. Sure to be one of the most talked about and influential volumes ever dedicated to the exploration of gay sex and sexuality. $12.95/424-0

A RICHARD KASAK BOOK

LARRY TOWNSEND
ASK LARRY
Starting just before the onslaught of AIDS, Townsend wrote the "Leather Notebook" column for *Drummer* magazine. Now, readers can avail themselves of Townsend's collected wisdom, as well as the author's contemporary commentary—a careful consideration of the way life has changed in the AIDS era. Don't miss this ultimate reference volume. $12.95/289-2

CECILIA TAN, EDITOR
SM VISIONS: The Best of Circlet Press
"Fabulous books! There's nothing else like them."
—Susie Bright, *Best American Erotica* and *Herotica 3*
Circlet Press, the first publishing house to devote itself exclusively to the erotic science fiction and fantasy genre, is now represented by the best of its very best: *SM Visions*—sure to be one of the most thrilling and eye-opening rides through the erotic imagination ever published. $10.95/339-2

FELICE PICANO
DRYLAND'S END
The science fiction debut of the highly acclaimed author of *Men Who Loved Me* and *Like People in History*. Set five thousand years in the future, *Dryland's End* takes place in a fabulous techno-empire ruled by intelligent, powerful women. While the Matriarchy has ruled for over two thousand years and altered human language, thought and society, it is now unraveling. Military rivalries, religious fanaticism and economic competition threaten to destroy the mighty empire. $12.95/279-5

RANDY TUROFF, EDITOR
LESBIAN WORDS: State of the Art
One of the widest assortments of lesbian nonfiction writing in one revealing volume. Dorothy Allison, Jewelle Gomez, Judy Grahn, Eileen Myles, Robin Podolsky and many others are represented by some of their best work, looking at not only the current fashionability the media has brought to the lesbian "image," but important considerations of the lesbian past via historical inquiry and personal recollections. A fascinating, provocative volume. $10.95/340-6

MICHAEL ROWE
WRITING BELOW THE BELT: Conversations with Erotic Authors
Journalist Michael Rowe interviewed the best erotic writers—both those well-known for their work in the field and those just starting out—and presents the collected wisdom in *Writing Below the Belt*. Rowe speaks frankly with cult favorites such as Pat Califia, crossover success stories like John Preston, and up-and-comers Michael Lowenthal and Will Leber. A revealing volume dedicated to this overlooked genre. $19.95/363-5

EURYDICE
f/32
"It's wonderful to see a woman...celebrating her body and her sexuality by creating a fabulous and funny tale." —Kathy Acker
With the story of Ela (whose name is a pseudonym for orgasm), Eurydice won the National Fiction competition sponsored by Fiction Collective Two and Illinois State University. A funny, disturbing quest for unity, *f/32* prompted Frederic Tuten to proclaim "almost any page...redeems us from the anemic writing and banalities we have endured in the past decade..." $10.95/350-3

A RICHARD KASAK BOOK

RUSS KICK
OUTPOSTS:
A Catalog of Rare and Disturbing Alternative Information
A huge, authoritative guide to some of the most bizarre publications available today! Rather than simply summarize the plethora of opinions crowding the American scene, Kick has tracked down and compiled reviews of work penned by political extremists, conspiracy theorists, hallucinogenic pathfinders, sexual explorers, and others. Each review is followed by ordering information for the many readers sure to want these publications for themselves. $18.95/0202-8

WILLIAM CARNEY
THE REAL THING
Carney gives us a good look at the mores and lifestyle of the first generation of gay leathermen. A chilling mystery/romance novel as well. —Pat Califia

With a new introduction by Michael Bronski. Out of print for years, *The Real Thing* has long served as a touchstone in any consideration of gay "edge fiction." First published in 1968, this uncompromising story of New York leathermen received instant acclaim. Out of print for years, *The Real Thing* returns, ready to thrill a new generation. $10.95/280-9

MICHAEL LASSELL
THE HARD WAY
Lassell is a master of the necessary word. In an age of tepid and whining verse, his bawdy and bittersweet songs are like a plunge in cold champagne. —Paul Monette

The first collection of renowned gay writer Michael Lassell's poetry, fiction and essays. As much a chronicle of post-Stonewall gay life as a compendium of a remarkable writer's work. $12.95/231-0

AMARANTHA KNIGHT, EDITOR
LOVE BITES
A volume of tales dedicated to legend's sexiest demon—the Vampire. Includes such names as Ron Dee, Nancy A. Collins, Nancy Kilpatrick, Lois Tilton and David Aaron Clark. Not only the finest collection of erotic horror available—but a virtual who's who of promising new talent. A must for fans of both the horror and erotic genres. $12.95/234-5

LOOKING FOR MR. PRESTON
Edited by Laura Antoniou, *Looking for Mr. Preston* includes work by Lars Eighner, Pat Califia, Michael Bronski, Joan Nestle, and others who contributed interviews, essays and personal reminiscences of John Preston—a man whose career spanned the industry. Preston was the author of over twenty books, and edited many more. Ten percent of the proceeds from sale of the book will go to the AIDS Project of Southern Maine, for which Preston served as President of the Board. $23.95/288-4

MICHAEL LOWENTHAL, EDITOR
THE BEST OF THE BADBOYS
A collection of the best of Masquerade Books' phenomenally popular Badboy line of gay erotic writing. The very best of the leading Badboys is collected here, in this testament to the artistry that has catapulted these "outlaw" authors to bestselling status. John Preston, Aaron Travis, Larry Townsend, John Rowberry, Clay Caldwell and Lars Eighner are here represented by their most provocative writing. Michael Lowenthal both edited this remarkable collection and provides the Introduction. $12.95/233-7

A RICHARD KASAK BOOK

GUILLERMO BOSCH
RAIN

An adult fairy tale, *Rain* takes place in a time when the mysteries of Eros are played out against a background of uncommon deprivation. The tale begins on the 1,537th day of drought—when one man comes to know the true depths of thirst. In a quest to sate his hunger for some knowledge of the wide world, he is taken through a series of extraordinary, unearthly encounters that promise to change not only his life, but the course of civilization around him.   A haunting and provocative debut. $12.95/232-9

LUCY TAYLOR
UNNATURAL ACTS

"A topnotch collection..." —Science Fiction Chronicle

A remarkable debut volume from an acclaimed writer. *Unnatural Acts* plunges deep into the dark side of the psyche, far past all pleasantries and prohibitions, and brings to life a disturbing vision of erotic horror. Unrelenting angels and hungry gods play with souls and bodies in Taylor's murky cosmos: where heaven and hell are merely differences of perspective; where redemption and damnation lie behind the same shocking acts. A frightening look at human desire. $12.95/181-0

SAMUEL R. DELANY
THE MOTION OF LIGHT IN WATER

"A very moving, intensely fascinating literary biography from an extraordinary writer. Thoroughly admirable candor and luminous stylistic precision; the artist as a young man and a memorable picture of an age."   —William Gibson

Award-winning author Samuel R. Delany's riveting autobiography covers the early years of one of science fiction's most important voices. Delany paints a vivid and compelling picture of New York's East Village in the early '60s—a time of unprecedented social transformation. *The Motion of Light in Water* traces the roots of one of America's most innovative writers. $12.95/133-0

THE MAD MAN

For his thesis, graduate student John Marr researches the life and work of the brilliant Timothy Hasler: a philosopher whose career was cut tragically short over a decade earlier. Marr soon begins to believe that Hasler's death might hold some key to his own life as a gay man in the age of AIDS.

What Delany has done here is take the ideas of the Marquis de Sade one step further, by filtering extreme and obsessive sexual behavior through the sieve of post-modern experience....   —Lambda Book Report

Delany develops an insightful dichotomy between [his protagonist]'s two worlds: the one of cerebral philosophy and dry academia, the other of heedless, 'impersonal' obsessive sexual extremism. When these worlds finally collide ... the novel achieves a surprisingly satisfying resolution....   —Publishers Weekly $23.95/193-4/hardcover

KATHLEEN K.
SWEET TALKERS

Kathleen K., a highly successful businesswoman, opens up her diary for a rare peek at her day-to-day life. What makes Kathleen's story unusual is the nature of her business. Kathleen K. is a popular phone sex operator—and she now reveals a number of secrets and surprises. Far from being a sleazy, underground scam, the service Kathleen provides often speaks to the lives of its customers with a compassion they receive nowhere else. A revealing look into this increasingly popular form of entertainment. $12.95/192-6

A RICHARD KASAK BOOK

ROBERT PATRICK
TEMPLE SLAVE

You must read this book. —Quentin Crisp

This is nothing less than the secret history of the most theatrical of theaters, the most bohemian of Americans and the most knowing of queens. Patrick writes with a lush and witty abandon, as if this departure from the crafting of plays has energized him. Temple Slave is also one of the best ways to learn what it was like to be fabulous, gay, theatrical and loved in a time at once more and less dangerous to gay life than our own. —Genre

$12.95/191-8

DAVID MELTZER
THE AGENCY TRILOGY

...'The Agency' is clearly Meltzer's paradigm of society; a mindless machine of which we are all 'agents,' including those whom the machine supposedly serves....

—Norman Spinrad

With the Essex House edition of *The Agency* in 1968, the highly regarded poet David Meltzer took America on a trip into a hell of unbridled sexuality. The story of a supersecret, Orwellian sexual network, *The Agency* explored issues of erotic dominance and submission with an immediacy and frankness previously unheard of in American literature, as well as presented a vision of an America consumed and dehumanized by a lust for power. $12.95/216-7

SKIN TWO
THE BEST OF *SKIN TWO* Edited by Tim Woodward

For over a decade, *SKIN TWO* has served the international fetish community as a groundbreaking journal from the crossroads of sexuality, fashion, and art. *SKIN TWO* specializes in provocative, challenging essays by the finest writers working in the "radical sex" scene. Collected here are the articles and interviews that established the magazine's reputation. Including interviews with cult figures Tim Burton, Clive Barker and Jean Paul Gaultier. $12.95/130-6

JOHN PRESTON
MY LIFE AS A PORNOGRAPHER
And Other Indecent Acts

...essential and enlightening...His sex-positive stand on safer-sex education as the only truly effective AIDS-prevention strategy will certainly not win him any conservative converts, but AIDS activists will be shouting their assent.... [My Life as a Pornographer] *is a bridge from the sexually liberated 1970s to the more cautious 1990s, and Preston has walked much of that way as a standard-bearer to the cause for equal rights....* —Library Journal

My Life as a Pornographer...*is not pornography, but rather reflections upon the writing and production of it. In a deeply sex-phobic world, Preston has never shied away from a vision of the redemptive potential of the erotic drive. Better than perhaps anyone in our community, Preston knows how physical joy can bridge differences and make us well.*
—Lambda Book Report $12.95/135-7

HUSTLING:
A Gentleman's Guide to the Fine Art of Homosexual Prostitution

A must-read for any man who's ever considered selling IT, either to make ends meet, or just for fun. John Preston solicited the advice of "working boys" from across the country in his effort to produce the ultimate guide to the hustler's world.

...fun and highly literary. What more could you expect from such an accomplished activist, author and editor? —Drummer $12.95/137-3

ORDERING IS EASY!

MC/VISA orders can be placed by calling our toll-free number
PHONE 800-375-2356 / FAX 212 986-7355
or mail this coupon to:
**MASQUERADE DIRECT
DEPT. BMMQ66, 801 2ND AVE., NY, NY 10017**

BUY ANY FOUR BOOKS AND CHOOSE ONE ADDITIONAL BOOK, OF EQUAL OR LESSER VALUE, AS YOUR FREE GIFT.

QTY.	TITLE	NO.	PRICE
			FREE
			FREE

BMMQ66 SUBTOTAL
POSTAGE and HANDLING

We Never Sell, Give or Trade Any Customer's Name. **TOTAL**

In the U.S., please add $1.50 for the first book and 75¢ for each additional book; in Canada, add $2.00 for the first book and $1.25 for each additional book. Foreign countries: add $4.00 for the first book and $2.00 for each additional book. No C.O.D. orders. Please make all checks payable to Masquerade Books. Payable in U.S. currency only. New York state residents add 8.25% sales tax. Please allow 4-6 weeks for delivery.

NAME

ADDRESS

CITY _____ STATE _____ ZIP _____

TEL ( )

PAYMENT: ☐ CHECK   ☐ MONEY ORDER   ☐ VISA   ☐ MC

CARD NO. _____ EXP. DATE _____